THE TREE POACHERS

based on true events

THE TREE POACHERS

A NOVEL

zach boldt

Copyright © 2024 Zach Boldt

All rights reserved. No part of this publication may be reproduced, stored, or transmitted in any form or by any means, electronic, mechanical, photocopying, recording, scanning, or otherwise without written permission from the publisher. It is illegal to copy this book, post it to a website, or distribute it by any other means without permission.

This novel is a work of fiction and is based on true events. These events have been fictionalized to various degrees for various reasons. The names, characters, and incidents portrayed in it are the work of the author's imagination. Any resemblance to actual people, living or dead, is entirely coincidental.

Neither this book nor its author is affiliated with Redwood National Park.

Text © 2024 Zach Boldt

Cover Art © 2024 Rudy Manninger

ISBN 9798321217252

First edition paperback, independently published through Amazon KDP.

For Mark, Bob and Wade of Distractible

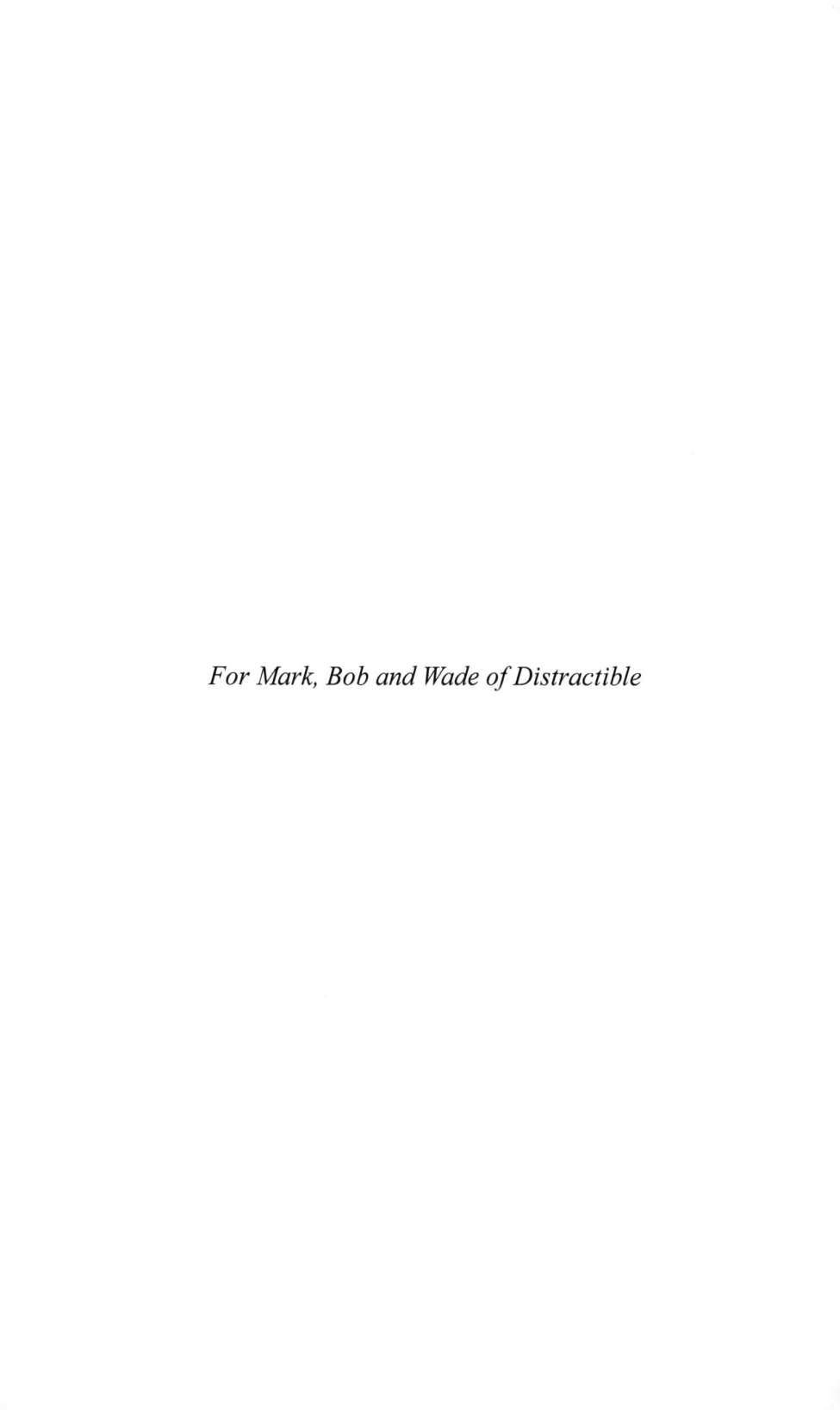

I

WHEN SHIT HITS THE FAN

1

THE HEIST

They snuck like elephants through the evening, barely caring that their heavy footfalls snapped twigs and crushed the dead vegetation that littered the forest floor. The sun fell in the sky, painting the trees with a tangerine hue and projecting the men's shadows across the ground. Each one held onto a long rope, the limp sections between them flopping up and down. Grayson's shovel clanked against the trunk of a tree, sending a ring like a church bell's through the quiet woods. Darren turned around from the front and glared, holding a finger to his lips while Grayson stuffed the shovel's metal head under his armpit to stop its ringing. "Dumb fuck," Darren muttered under his breath.

The crew arrived at the tree five minutes later, leaving them almost no time to cut the burl and start hauling it away. They would be halfway out of the forest by the time the rangers got to the tree, but if Cherry's math was correct, dragging the heavy burl would slow them down and narrow the gap between them and the rangers. "Possibly to the point of capture," Cherry had said. And if that happened, Darren would scream everyone's ears off on the way to the police station.

Cherry moved to the front of the line and waited for Darren's signal to rev up the chainsaw. He brought the blade to the top of the burl and began cutting through the redwood. The sawdust shot from the tree and carried a sweet scent with it. Darren and Scrub winced at the chainsaw's mechanical scream, checking wildly over their shoulders for the beams of flashlights. The sun had cowered low enough below the horizon to cover the thieves in a layer of night. They left their flashlights in the truck as to not draw any more attention to themselves, effectively leaving them blind in a maze of trees. But it was a straight shot back to Vic and the truck. All they had to do was retrace their steps and they would be home free.

Cherry was just over halfway through the burl when Scrub saw a dim circle of light steady onto Darren's face. They crouched down immediately and motioned for Grayson to do the same. Instead, he jammed the shovel between the burl and the tree and pushed with his shoulder against the handle.

"Get down, Grayson!" Scrub yelled over the chainsaw.

"I'm trying to wedge it out!"

Grayson continued to throw himself at the shovel as the circle of light focused on Cherry and the tree. He stepped back a few feet to get a running start at it, but Darren stuck out his foot for Grayson to trip over. Grayson sprawled out on the ground, his head slamming down against the hard earth. Cherry looked frantically at Darren and Scrub, down to Grayson, the roar of the chainsaw quieting for a moment.

"Keep cutting!" Darren screamed, reaching into the back of his waistband. "We're getting this one!"

Cherry did as he was told while Darren wrapped his hand around the grip of his pistol. "Why do they always have to catch us?" He looked at Scrub, flicked the safety off, and sighed. "We have to slow them down somehow."

Indistinct yells began accompanying the light, the barks of the rangers and the chainsaw melding together into one awful sound. Scrub looked from Darren to Cherry, who had cut nearly the whole burl off the tree. Scrub looked back to Darren, who had taken cover behind a nearby shrub and aimed his pistol toward the rangers. Finally, Scrub looked to Grayson, still on the ground. He checked for a pulse in Grayson's wrist and determined he was still alive. Scrub began lightly slapping Grayson in the face, trying to wake him up, the slaps growing more forceful when Grayson didn't wake up. Scrub stopped slapping him altogether once the shooting started.

Darren sent the first shot off as a warning, but the rangers returned fire with surprisingly good accuracy. Bullets were exchanged, one of them barely missing Cherry's head as it lodged itself into the tree behind him. "Fuck, okay," he said to Scrub, putting the chainsaw down. "Pull this thing off."

Scrub left Grayson and went to Cherry's aid, taking one end of the rope and tying it around the burl. Once the knot was secure, Cherry and Scrub took their places along the rope and pulled. Pops rang through the air from both the guns and the burl, the ones from the guns getting increasingly louder. Scrub planted his feet and tugged the rope hard, the cords in his neck straining. With that, the burl snapped off the tree and thumped into the dirt.

"Darren!" Scrub yelled. "It's off, come on!"

Darren put his gun away and hustled to the rope. He picked up the loose end and heaved, making the burl tumble to him. Cherry helped him while Scrub's eyes scanned Grayson. "We can't leave him," Scrub said.

"Why not?" Darren huffed.

"You know he's gonna talk if they catch him."

"Look at him! He probably got amnesia from that fall, just come and help us!"

"We can't leave him!"

Darren threw down the rope and stomped to Scrub. "Fine, then." He retrieved his gun and shoved it into Scrub's chest. "Shoot him. So he won't talk." Darren went back to the rope and started pulling. Cherry was strung along with him, not making eye contact with Scrub. He just shook his head and followed Darren, picking up the chainsaw before he left.

Scrub clutched the gun, hands shaking. He tried to control his breathing, going through some exercise he'd heard his mom do after therapy. It was no use, though; with all the sounds melding together, he couldn't think straight. In a haze, Scrub looked at Grayson's motionless body. *He's already dead*, he thought to himself. *This won't hurt him at all. He can't feel anything if he's already dead.*

Scrub took a deep breath as he aimed and squeezed the trigger, a loud bang ripping through the forest as he took off after Darren and Cherry.

II

BEFORE SHIT HITS THE FAN

2

FORTY-THREE YEARS BEFORE

Shit shit shit shit shit.

Gary's sawing was a lot louder than he thought it would be. The whole process was louder than he thought it would be. He walked through the forest over dead leaves and twigs that crunched with every step. The night breeze whipped around the trees and rustled the forest floor, his own breath hissed into the darkness. It started shaking when he realized this would take a long time. A *really* long time.

Shit shit shit shit shit. This isn't going to work. Shit!

Why did he think he could do this alone? He was stupid to ever think that he could. His tiny saw against the Giantess. It would take hours, maybe days for him to cut it alone! Why was he even doing this? It wasn't too late to turn back. But he already made the trek out here; what would be the point if he just turned around? His whole cause would crumble, as he would probably never get this lucky again. This was his only chance to get revenge. But was this the way to do it?

And why was the tree female? How did that make any sense?

The damage to the tree was extensive, even in his first minutes of cutting. Gary huffed, almost stopping to give his body a break, but knew he didn't have the time. Every second counted now, and he would keep cutting for as long as it took, even if his arms fell off. As he sawed deeper and deeper into the tree, Gary began to think that the loss of extremities could be possible.

But his physical anguish turned emotional when he remembered exactly why he was doing this. Gary had been accepted into Redwood National Park's ranger program in its inception. When he arrived for his first day of training, he came to find out that the other junior rangers were far younger than him, some looking as young as teenagers. When he asked his overseer how young the others were, he got answers ranging from nineteen to twenty-five. Gary was forty-six.

It became increasingly obvious to both Gary and his overseer that he was not cut out for life as a park ranger. The main problem was his distaste for bugs, which there were a lot of out in the redwood forest. Gary would let out a yelp every time one crawled across his path, the sound disturbing the ecosystem of the park as well as his compatriots. Despite his profuse apologies, he was ultimately let go from the ranger program. "You just don't have it in you," his overseer said. "But you're welcome to apply for one of our janitorial positions."

Janitorial positions, Gary thought. *Yeah, there'll be need for cleanup after I'm done here.*

The Giantess was the park's main draw for tourists right from the start. People from all across the country flocked to bear witness to the 340-foot-tall redwood tree. A lot of them came for the sole purpose of hugging her, claiming that by doing it they would have a better connection with nature and be healed by her. Most of those people reeked of skunk and drove Volkswagen buses. Nevertheless, a theory circulated through park visitors that the Giantess was the physical body of Mother Nature herself.

And Gary was cutting into her ankles, hoping to get deep enough to topple her.

He continued sawing, now sweating in his flannel shirt and breathing more heavily than before. His saw blade was nearly buried in the trunk of the tree when Gary felt something on his hand. He brushed it off, but in doing so he lost balance in his crouched stance and fell backwards, catching himself just as he was about to hit the ground. Before he was able to situate himself, Gary took notice of the sandy texture beneath his right palm. The sensation that came after was much, much worse.

Henry heard the scream over everything else. It traveled through the trees, the walls of the ranger cabin, and his headphones, which were blasting rock music. At first he thought it was mixed into the song, something he hadn't picked up on until this listen, but when he paused his music, the screaming continued. It sounded distant, meaning it probably came from the forest. Why did the teens always have to sneak in when he was on night duty? Fairly fresh out of high school himself, Henry understood the appeal behind the idea: going into a spooky forest in the middle of the night, hunting for ghosts and other creatures—but why did they have to make it *his* problem?

Henry removed his headphones and stood up from the desk before putting on his hat and tightening his utility belt. He pulled his revolver from his holster, made sure it was loaded, and replaced it. He thought back to the training process with the guns they were using, how long they spent on safety, wondering why he would ever need to shoot anyone, much less carry a gun with him at all times. Henry vowed that unless a person or the park was in imminent danger, he would never use his revolver to its full potential. Until then, he'd merely brandish it, aiming it at the person with the safety on at most. He hoped he wouldn't have to do more than that as he left the cabin, turning off the light and locking the door behind him.

The main trail through the park started immediately beside the ranger's cabin, a sign with arrows pointing to different attractions between them. The trail broke off into forks that led to the Ring, the Grove, and the Giantess. In the months of Henry's employment, having witnessed multiple cases of public indecency, he determined that the Grove was a hotspot for people wanting to become more "connected to nature." However, when he took the fork in the trail to get to the wide open spot in the forest, he found nothing but a young deer drinking from the stream. Henry backtracked and made his way toward the Ring of redwood trees, but stopped when he heard some rustling coming from the direction of the Giantess. He slid his flashlight out of his utility belt and flicked it on, a dim circle of light shining into the forest. It bounced around with his shaking hands, not brought on by the brisk night but by his nerves.

Keep it together, Henry. You're not a kid anymore, you're not afraid of the dark.

But he was lying to himself. He was alone in the middle of one of the most expansive forests in the country at dead of night. The moon and his flashlight did little to bring Henry comfort. Ironically, the firearm at his hip was the thing that put him at ease. At least he could protect himself against whatever he found—or whatever found him. As that thought crossed his mind, Henry put his free hand around the grip of his revolver.

The rustling intensified as Henry approached the Giantess, the beam from his flashlight shuddering more than ever. He gasped as it landed on the base of the massive tree, seeing the handle of a saw sticking out of a haphazard incision about three feet from the roots of the tree. Before becoming a ranger, Henry wasn't one to go out of his way to save the environment. It's not like he littered every chance he got, but he certainly didn't picket outside government buildings demanding that the new oil pipeline stop construction through whatever forest they were tearing down. Now, having worked around these trees for almost two years, seeing them and their glory every day, neck pain galore from bending upwards and marveling their breathtaking size, his outlook on them—and nature as a whole—changed substantially.

In the ground next to the tree was a large anthill, its occupants swarming outside of it, trying to mitigate the damages caused by the hand that made the indent in the sand. Henry could hear fast breathing coming from the other side of the tree. His own breath quickened as he rounded the trunk, his light falling on an older man sitting catatonic against the tree.

"Hey!" Henry said. "What are you doing here? The park's closed!"

The man's eyes stared forward, unblinking.

"Sir, are you alright? What happened here? Did you saw into the tree?"

"The ants," the man breathed. "They were all over me."

"Ants? Sir, are you alright?"

Finally, the man turned his head to face Henry. His skin was pale and his body shook with fear, and in that moment, Henry recognized him. Although the time he knew the man was brief, he knew the scream sounded familiar. "Mr. Gerschult?"

The man squinted at Henry and then got a disgusted look on his face. "Oh, of course," Mr. Gerschult said. "Of course I get caught by one of the children they decided to hire over me!"

"Mr. Gerschult, what are you doing out here? What have you done to the Giantess?"

The man sighed and stood up. "Call me Gary."

"Okay, Gary. Now would you like to tell me what happened here?"

Gary swayed. Henry wondered if he might have been drinking, but smelled no alcohol on him. "I wanted," said Gary, "to get back at them. At you."

"This was not the way to do it. You realize you'll go to jail for this, right?"

"Yeah..." He looked down at the saw in the tree. "But only if you're alive to tell someone."

Henry once again found his hand gripping his gun. "Gary, whatever you're thinking about doing, don't."

Gary grunted and lunged downward, ripping the saw from the tree and slashing at Henry with it. Before he could get his gun out, the saw caught Henry's arm and cut deep, white hot pain shooting through the wound. Despite his injury, he was able to distance himself from the madman. Henry pulled his revolver from his holster and aimed it at Gary, skipping his first step of brandishing in hopes that Gary would put the saw down and cooperate. But, once again, Henry was lying to himself and Gary continued to pursue him with the saw. He had no choice.

For the first time in his career, Henry clicked the safety off on his revolver and pulled the trigger.

3

ONE YEAR AND THREE MONTHS BEFORE

In terms of closeness to family, Sam's uncle Darren had always been at the bottom of his list. His dad's brother was a mystery, never showing an ounce of interest in Sam's life—or anyone's life, for that matter. The only way they could get him to come to Christmas was to send a picture of whatever alcohol was in the host's house, and even then, if Darren didn't like what was on the menu, he wouldn't be attending. He was constantly absent from any sort of family event. Holidays, birthdays, reunions, you name it, he wasn't there. So, naturally, Sam was surprised to see Darren standing in the corner of the room at his dad's memorial service.

Sam didn't dare let his mom know Darren was here; she would be on the man in no time. Plus, she was already going through enough stress with the loss of her husband. Sam took the route of discretion as he crossed the floor to the back of the funeral home where his uncle stood, leaning against the wall on his arm that wasn't in a sling.

"Hey there, Sam," Darren said, a smile on his face. "How have you been? Man, I haven't seen you in so long. You grew so much!"

"What are you doing here?" Sam asked.

"I am paying respects to my brother, of course. Why else would I be here?"

"To get a rise out of the rest of the family. You know that they—"

"They all hate me. Yes, I'm aware."

Sam sighed. He wasn't distant from Darren entirely by choice. Sam's mother was insistent on keeping him away from her impressionable son, ever since Darren had picked him up from school one day in first grade. He'd let Sam, a six year old, sit in the front seat, and subjected him to the auditory torture that was early-2000s death metal. After only ten seconds of the first song, Sam was in tears, wondering why the man on the radio was screaming so loud.

"You will never pick him up again," Sam's mother had told Darren.

"It's not my fault you guys never showed him the good stuff," Darren replied. "I let him in on all the hot new tracks."

"He listens to nursery rhymes, Darren! He barely knows the alphabet!"

Sam had felt bad for his uncle's detachment from the family ever since he gained a sense of empathy. But now, when Darren was showing his face for the sole purpose of pissing people off, Sam couldn't care less about him. "Get out."

"Sam, I wanted to talk to you—"

"You had plenty of opportunities to do that before now, and

you didn't take them. I'm letting you off easy. If my mother catches you here, you're done for."

Darren's demeanor shifted like a mouse's as it's being chased by a cat. Sam could tell that his threat struck a nerve, even before Darren nervously scampered away from his corner. He left the funeral home, snatching a slice of cheese from the charcuterie board on his way out. Sam watched his uncle through the window, shuffling to his truck at the back of the parking lot. As Darren sped away, Sam felt a hand on his shoulder.

"What are you doing over here?" his mother asked. "Who were you talking to?"

Sam turned from the window toward his mom. "No one," he said. "I was just making sure there was enough meat and cheese left out here."

Even though his dad was dead, Sam still had to go to school. That wasn't what he had expected, because in every movie he'd ever seen, the person with the dead parent would get weeks off school at a time. Some of them even had their grades bumped up a whole letter. That's what Sam needed right now; biology wasn't looking too good for him, and if he didn't want to take it again in his senior year, he'd need to either study harder or kill his mom for another letter grade. And even though the year—and thus his chance to up his grades—was almost over, he wasn't too keen on the second option.

So there Sam sat in biology, listening to his teacher talking about trees.

"Isn't it interesting," Mr. Veranda said, "that trees at the equator don't have any rings to tell us how old they are? Why would that be? Does anyone know?"

The question was met with indifference and a cough from the back of the class. Sam raised his hand, almost sure his answer would be wrong.

"Yes, Sam?"

"There are no seasonal changes at the equator."

Mr. Veranda nodded. "Therefore..."

"Therefore trees grow at the same rate all year round."

"That's right! You see, depending on temperature, a tree will grow at different rates, slower when cold and faster when warm. That's what gives a tree's rings different colors. Good work, Sam."

As Mr. Veranda clicked to the next slide of the presentation, Sam felt a surge of pride go through his body. In his peripheral vision, he could see the guy sitting in the desk next to him roll his eyes. Sam pursed his lips and scrawled down the information on the slide while Mr. Veranda recited it aloud.

"Now, onto a most interesting topic," he started. He said every topic was an interesting topic, but Sam could barely keep himself concentrated on any of them. "So, let's say that you're riding your bike one day, and you forgot to tie your shoe before getting on."

A girl in front of Sam raised her hand and Mr. Veranda called on her. "I only ride my bike in flip-flops," she said.

"Great, but not my point. Your lace gets stuck in the chain, you skid to a stop, and topple over on the pavement. Your knee is scraped up pretty bad, and your mom is definitely going to have to hold you down while she douses your wound in isopropyl alcohol. Anyway, after a while, what happens to that scrape on your knee?"

"It hurts like a bitch," someone said from behind Sam.

The class erupted into laughter and Mr. Veranda reprimanded the kid for using such crass language. "Other than that, your body will build a protective layer around it until the skin beneath heals completely. That's a scab. A tree practically does the same thing whenever it experiences trauma, which can come from fungi, viruses, or direct, abrasive contact. However, rather than falling off after it has healed, the scab will grow into something called a burl."

Mr. Veranda clicked to the next slide, which had two pictures on it. One was of a tree with a growth the size of a basketball on its trunk. The other was what looked to be a stump, but looked much glossier and pretty than a normal stump would.

"These are some pretty gnarly burls that were cut from a maple tree. Now, obviously, that picture of the burl while it's still on the tree is not a nice sight, but that other picture is what the inside of a burl looks like. Because of its beauty and rarity, burl wood is extremely valuable. You've probably seen a product made with burl wood in passing. You might even have one in your own home."

On the next slide were two more pictures, one of an ornate wooden table and another of a vibrant red guitar. "These are just a few items that utilize the aesthetic of burl wood. That guitar is made partially from amboyna or narra wood. That's what gives it that cool red color."

The girl in front of Sam raised her hand again. He expected her to tell Mr. Veranda that she only played blue guitars, but instead asked a surprisingly insightful question that Sam himself didn't know the answer to.

"Can any tree grow a burl?"

"Yes!" Mr. Veranda was getting excited now. "However, they are more common in some trees than others."

"So redwood trees can grow burls?"

"Of course they can, and they have. Many of the trees in the Redwood National Park have burls on them."

"My mom took me on a tour there once," the guy next to Sam said. "They have a special tour route just for the messed-up trees. It was kinda cool."

"Cool indeed," Mr. Veranda said, clicking to the next slide. "Of course, you won't have to know *all* of that for the test, but just prepare yourselves to know what causes a burl to form on a tree."

Sam finished writing down the information about burls and then looked back up at the projector screen, waiting to jot down the next round of notes. In the back of his mind, something stirred up a memory of his father being infatuated with trees. There may have even been something in the memory about burls, but Sam brushed the thought away and chalked it up to association by coincidence. How wrong he was.

The final bell of the school year rang through the halls. Students scrambled out of their desks and flooded the areas around their lockers. Teachers followed them, trying to quell the chaos before it got out of hand, but their presence had little effect on the excited teenagers rampaging into their summer vacation.

Sam joined his locker neighbors in the revelry, high-fiving Bradley on his right before he threw a semester's worth of math homework into the garbage can. He was about to follow it up by tossing his biology notes, but something within him told him that he shouldn't. He thought back to what Mr. Veranda had said in their one-on-one meeting last week.

"I must say, Sam, I am very impressed with your work. Don't take this the wrong way, but I wasn't expecting this much quality from you, especially coming toward the end of the year. I am pleasantly surprised by your drive."

"Thank you, Mr. Veranda."

"Of course. I hope you take another science class with me before you graduate."

"I just might." And then Sam left the room.

Of course, Sam didn't have much interest in taking another science class. It wasn't because he didn't like Mr. Veranda; he was a fine teacher. Even though Sam wasn't sure where he wanted his life to go, he was certain he didn't want to do anything with biology. But instead of getting rid of the biology notebook, he stuffed it into his backpack. Bradley took notice of this. "Why are you keeping that?" he asked Sam.

"Oh, uh," Sam stuttered. "There's still some blank pages left. I figure I can get a little more use out of it."

"Ah. That's fair I guess. Save the trees."

"Yeah." Sam was about to leave, but Bradley tapped him on his arm.

"Yo, are you going to Ripp's party tonight?" he asked.

Sam didn't know Ripp, but he knew of him. They had a few classes together, and whenever Ripp spoke up in them, Sam was reminded of the kid who said that a knee scrape "hurt like a bitch." Still, Ripp's family was the richest in the school. Once for a class fundraiser, his father gave people helicopter rides over their town in exchange for charity money.

"Not sure," Sam replied. "When does it start?"

"Five. It's gonna be at his lake house. You know Perula road?"

He did. How could he not with all the outrageous party tales that happened in houses on that road? "Yeah."

"Swing by if you get the chance," Bradley said, closing his locker. "It's gonna be a rager." He waved goodbye to Sam and walked down the hallway, clapping one of his friends on the back.

Sam was leaning toward going to Ripp's party, which surprised him a little. He didn't think of himself as a party person, but it was a special occasion and he was feeling up for a good time. What he wasn't up for was asking his mother for permission to actually go to said party. She was super protective of him, barely letting him out of the house to hang out with friends. She even made him download a tracking app on his phone so she could see his location at all times. He made sure to research ways to disable it so she couldn't see where he was. Sam's mother insisted that she would only check it in emergency situations, but he knew she would sometimes stalk him on his way home from school.

But when he asked her about the party, albeit slowly and only revealing a few details at a time, Sam's mom was supportive of his wishes to get out of the house.

"Really?" Sam asked her.

"Yeah," his mother responded. "You stayed out of C range in all your classes. You deserve it."

"Awesome! Thank you so much!" Sam gave his mother a hug, then backed away. "I have another question."

"No, you cannot drive yourself. I will drop you off."

Sam sighed. He couldn't get dropped off by his mother! Everyone would think he was a dork! He bit the inside of his cheek, knowing that it would be impossible to change his mother's mind. She was already allowing him to go to the party, and he didn't want to test his luck with more arguing. So when Sam rolled up to Ripp's extravagant house, riding in the passenger seat of his mom's beater minivan, he reminded himself how fortunate he was to even be there at all.

"Call me if you want to get picked up early," his mother said. "Or if you need anything at all."

"I will," Sam said. He got out of the van and walked up the driveway as his mom pulled away from the curb. The brick-lined driveway wound up to the massive house at the top of the hill, sounds of partying echoing down to Sam's ears. He knew he couldn't show up early, because everyone would wonder how he got invited. He was sure to find Bradley first and stick close at his side; he was most likely the only person at Ripp's party that resembled a friend.

"Sam!" Bradley yelled when Sam found him. He could smell the alcohol on Bradley's breath. "So glad you came! You want something to drink? There's some beer in those coolers over there, sodas, water, you know."

"I'm fine for now, thanks," Sam said.

"Alright. Hey, I'm gonna go play pong in the backyard. You wanna come with me? I'll even drink for you if you want."

Sam nodded and followed Bradley to the beer pong table, which was surrounded by drunk teenagers watching the ongoing game. The team on the left side of the table had two cups set up in front of them, while the team on the right had eight. Even though Sam had never played beer pong before, he could tell that the team on the left was not in great shape. The game ended with the right team sinking their last two shots and the left team missing their redemption. The players met at the sides of the table and shook hands, then stumbled away into the crowd to let the next match begin.

Bradley and Sam stepped up to the right side of the table—Bradley insisted that the right side was his lucky side. Two other guys, one tall and one beefy, stood across from them and set up their cups. Bradley cracked open two cans of beer and distributed them throughout their own cups, then crushed the empty cans and threw them to the side. "That's gonna be you guys," he said to their opponents.

"Huh?" Beefcake asked.

"We're gonna crush you."

"Oh, uhh... nuh uh!"

And the game started. Sam and Tallboy played rock-paper-scissors to decide who shot first. Sam threw rock and the other guy threw scissors. Bradley handed Sam a ping pong ball and he took his first shot, the ball hitting the rim of the center cup and bouncing off the table. Bradley threw his ball and sunk it into the back-left cup.

"Yeah, see?" Bradley taunted as Tallboy drank. "Crushing. You."

Their opponents answered by making three shots in a row with Beefcake missing wide on their fourth.

"Ah, fuck," Bradley said. He gathered the three cups around him and started pouring them all into one.

"Hey, what are you doing?" Tallboy asked.

"My friend here isn't drinking tonight," Bradley explained.

"Nah, he's gotta. Thems the rules."

"Yeah!" Beefcake agreed.

"Look, guys—"

"No, it's fine," Sam said. "I'll drink my share."

"You sure?"

Sam nodded.

Bradley shrugged and slid the cup over to Sam. It was more beer than Sam thought it would be, but he drank half anyway. The taste was foul; his dad let him try it once when Sam was ten, and it was worse now than he remembered it being. He set the cup down in front of Bradley, who pounded it back with much less shuddering and dry-heaving than Sam.

It was their turn again. Bradley shot first and missed, then Sam actually made one and Beefcake had to drink. He could see the appeal to this game now, and as the crowd buzzed around him, he found himself having a little fun.

Beefcake and Tallboy both missed. Bradley made one, Sam missed, Tallboy drank. The game went on, Sam feeling more and more intoxicated with every sip he took. He wasn't sure if he was imagining things or not, but he swore he could feel the world spinning beneath his feet.

Sam and Bradley had three cups up on their side and needed to make both of their shots to win. Bradley shot first and sunk it, the crowd cheering as Beefcake drank his cup. Both he and Tallboy glared across the table at Sam, but he couldn't see them. He was laser-focused on the last cup while Bradley tried to calm the audience.

"Hey, quiet down! Sam's about to make history here!"

Sam composed himself, breathing slowly through his nose as he drew his arm back to take his shot. The ball soared through the air, spun around on the rim of the cup, and flew off to the side. The crowd groaned, throwing their hands up in anger while the balls were passed to Beefcake at Tallboy. They both made their shots and Tallboy cracked his knuckles before throwing his ball directly into Sam and Bradley's last cup.

"Fuck!" Bradley yelled. "Alright Sam, you got this."

"What?" Sam asked.

"You're making this redemption shot. Right now."

"I'm not making shit!"

"Yes, you are! You got this!"

"Bradley, I really don't think I should take this shot."

"Hey!" Tallboy yelled from the other side of the table. "Are you doing this or what?"

"Fuck off!" Bradley looked Sam in the eyes. "You got this."

Sam sighed and took the ping pong ball from Bradley. He lined up his shot, licked his lips, and missed horribly. The crowd cheered and jumped at the table, congratulating Beefcake and Tallboy on their victory.

"Sorry, man," Sam said.

"It's all good," Bradley said. "I should've taken it."

"And that, ladies and gentlemen, is what happens when you don't have a father to teach you beer pong!"

Sam turned toward the crowd. "Who said that?"

Tallboy faced him. "Me," he said, "what about it?"

Instead of answering, Sam walked over to the other side of the table and grabbed the last cup on Tallboy's side. Before he could react, Tallboy was splashed with a face full of beer, followed by the empty plastic cup slapping him on the side of his head.

"Ah, shit," he said, wiping his face, "my eyes! You fucking asshole!" Tallboy lunged at Sam and put him in a headlock, which Sam was able to weasel out of before his windpipe got crushed. He ran away from the crowd toward the front of the house, pulling his phone from his pocket and trying to dial his mother's number. Before he could press the call button, his legs were swept out from under him and he hit the ground hard, the wind getting knocked out of his lungs. Tallboy loomed over him, about to land a punch into Sam's stomach, when someone Sam couldn't see ran out and broke up the fight.

"Cory, what the hell?"

"He threw beer at me, Ripp!"

"Who even is this fool?" Ripp asked.

Sam heard Bradley's voice nearby. "I invited him. But Ripp, you gotta understand—"

"Brad, no. This is a total party foul!"

"Cory made fun of his dad!"

Finally, Sam was able to roll over and look up. Ripp was the perfect mixture of Beefy and Tallboy, the latter's name ending up being Cory. Ripp looked down at Sam with a gentle yet scornful expression. "You good, bro?"

Sam gave a shaky thumbs-up and started getting to his feet. He looked to Bradley, hoping he would help him up, but he didn't. Sam turned to Cory, beer still dripping off his face. "I'm sorry about that," Sam said, the apology not even half-hearted.

"Yeah, whatever."

Cory brushed him off and Sam was livid. How could he be such a dick? At least Sam was nice enough to fake empathy. Cory just didn't give a shit.

"I'm gonna go," Sam said.

Nobody protested. He thought at least Bradley might speak up, tell him to stay and party some more, but even he was silent.

Sam left the party and walked back down the driveway, calling his mom on the way. While he waited at the curb, he heard the rev of an engine in the distance followed by police sirens. The sounds got louder and, eventually, the vehicles making them came into view. A rusty orange truck sped past Sam, the tarp in the bed of the truck flapping behind it. The police were close behind, lights and sirens blaring as they chased after the truck. Sam wasn't sure, but he thought he heard gunshots as the cars disappeared over a hill. But followed by all of that was Sam's mom, pulling up in her minivan to take her son home.

4

TEN MONTHS BEFORE

He blinked once and was in a different place. Darren felt like he was either falling or floating. He couldn't determine which, only that he wasn't touching the ground. His feet landed on something uneven, causing him to stumble a bit as he got used to the terrain. It took less effort this time, because this was his fourth or fifth time coming here in the past week. He didn't do it on purpose; why would he? Every time they got a hit, Darren was sure that it was far, far away from this spot. And yet, here he is, with no recollection of how.

There was stirring behind him and Darren whirled around, the ground crackling underneath his feet. He saw him leaning against the tree, a bullet hole in his chest. None of the distinguishing features on his face were present. It was as if skin grew over his eyes, nose, and mouth. Still, somehow, he screamed for help.

"I can't," Darren said. "I can't help you."

He blinked again and he was back in his bed, sitting upright and coated with sweat. He looked over at his alarm clock and saw that fifteen minutes had passed since he last checked. Darren sighed and laid back down, trying to get as comfortable as possible despite that awful image in his head. He'd been there before. But he was never like *that*.

Darren blinked once more and it was nine in the morning. The sun shone through the slats over his bedroom window, streaks of illuminated dust floating in the air. His sweat had soaked into the sheet under him and was now wet and cold. It was enough to rouse Darren from the bed, the earliest he had gotten up in months.

It seemed no one else was awake yet. The kitchen, in which Cherry normally made his breakfast in the early hours of the morning, sat exactly the same as they'd left it last night. Cans and bottles scattered across the counter. Darren's glass pipe sitting in the middle of the table like a junkie centerpiece. The whole place smelled awful, a mixture of fumes that should probably be toxic. Thanks to his habitual consumption of smokable drugs, Darren boasted that he had lungs of steel. "Until the cancer gets me," he would say, right before taking another hit of whatever happened to be in the pipe.

He swept the trash from the counter into the garbage can and then got a paper plate out of the cabinet. Darren was disappointed by the sparse options of food in the fridge—Vic would have to go shopping again soon—and reluctantly decided on a sandwich for breakfast for the third day in a row. He used the last of the bread and put a sizable dent in their ham and cheese supply. Darren pulled up a stool to the counter and hunched over his sandwich, his chewing the only sound he heard in the lonely kitchen.

As Darren ate, his mind wandered to the dream he'd woken up from. He had the same dream after every hit they made. It never strayed too far from the source material; the man was always sitting limp against the tree, bleeding out, begging for help. But this was the first time Darren had seen the man without a face. It was also the first time he thought about him as "the man" instead of his name, which he couldn't quite remember at the moment. Before he could reach back and find that information, Cherry walked into the kitchen, groaning and rubbing his face. "Morning," he said.

"Hey," Darren replied, taking another bite of his sandwich. "You look rough."

"Fuck you." Cherry grabbed the almost-empty bottle of orange juice out of the fridge and finished it off, then carefully placed the bottle on top of the mountain of bottles and cans in the garbage can. "You look rougher."

"Yeah, well..." Darren thought about telling Cherry about his dream. After all, he would understand more than anyone. But he decided against it, fearing Cherry might think he was crazy. "No more smoking before bed."

"I hope that's just for you, because I *only* smoke before bed." Cherry laughed and sat across from Darren at the counter. "You want some help today?"

"My shoulder is killing me. Do you even have to ask?"

"Okay. When's our buyer coming?"

"Three days."

"Boy, he doesn't give us a lot of time to get it ready, huh?"

Darren nodded. "We always get it done, though."

"Right. I'll be in the shop. Join me whenever."

Cherry left the house, leaving Darren alone once again. He ate the rest of his sandwich and threw away his paper plate, balancing it on top of the empty orange juice bottle. There was no doubt in his mind that the garbage would collapse before he even got out of the house, but he didn't care. *Leave it to Vic,* Darren thought as he passed the overflowing bin.

Darren ripped open the shop door, the old thing creaking terribly on its hinges. He'd always found it annoying that the door had to be practically wrestled with to open, but such is the case with old properties like his. And although he was in possession of large amounts of wood—"Enough to make a lumberjack jizz himself," he always said—there was no way he would waste it on replacing the door. That, and he just didn't feel like it.

The shop was tidier than normal; tools put away, extension cords wrapped and on the wall. Even the chop saw was set to standby, the blade guard down and the machine itself unplugged. Cherry must have whipped the place into shape for the new arrival. It was the only sign that he had been here.

"Cherry?" Darren called.

"I'm out back."

Darren went to the far side of the shop and found the garage door wide open. Cherry stood in the bed of the truck, folding up the tarp that covered it. "Doesn't look damaged," he said.

"Good. Get her down here."

"Should I just roll it out?"

"Yeah, she's strong enough."

Cherry bent down and pushed the hunk of wood to the open tailgate, then gave it a final shove with his foot and it thudded on the ground. This one was smaller than their previous bounty, and it wasn't even redwood. It had been almost too easy to get. It probably wouldn't be worth much. Still, Darren insisted that they cut it. After all, they hadn't made a sale in months, and money was running low. Everyone was desperate; he just hoped that their buyers were more desperate for inventory than he was for cash.

Darren surveyed the burl, pulled out his tape measure and spanned it across the widest part of the wood. "How big did they want it?"

"I want to say two feet," Cherry replied, "but I can't be sure."

Darren sighed. "We have two-foot-two here. Not much room for error."

"Let's just do it right the first time, then."

"We can only hope."

🌲

Fall was the second busiest season for Redwood National Park, right behind summer. Populations were diminishing now, the summer crowd going back home as the temperatures cooled off. The ice cream and tank tops were replaced by pumpkin spice and flannels, green leaves shifting to beautiful reds, oranges, and yellows. The fall crowd was more mellow than its summer counterpart, mostly composed of older families and couples rather than young people taking rampant hikes in the forest.

Denny worked the desk at the cabin on the first day of the fall season, handling admissions and pointing people toward different attractions around the park. It was no surprise to him that he was working in the cabin again; his work ethic and charm were too good to go to waste elsewhere. He never let a line form in front of his desk and got people whatever they needed, maps, merchandise, or otherwise.

A family of four came through the cabin door, the wife walking up to Denny's desk while the husband hung back with his daughters.

"Hi," she said, "we're here on vacation. It was supposed to be nice and relaxing, but we just keep fighting over what to check out first! This park is so big!"

"Right, so big!" Denny said, matching the woman's enthusiasm. "Have you heard of the Grove?"

"No, I don't think I have."

"It's this beautiful little huddle of nature in the forest. It's not too long of a walk, but even if it was, the view would be worth it."

"I see." She turned back to her family and her husband nodded his head. "Girls, what do you say?"

"I don't wanna walk anymore!" one of them yelled. "My feet hurt and I feel icky!"

Denny stood up and walked over to a picture on the wall. He beckoned the girl over, but she didn't budge. Her father had to take her by the hand and drag her over to Denny. "You see these flowers?" Denny asked her, pointing to the picture.

The girl looked at the picture and her demeanor shifted from annoyance to wonder. "They're pretty," she said.

"They grow in the Grove. There's a whole bunch of them out there. Do you want to see them in real life?"

The girl nodded emphatically and turned to her mother. "Can we go, mommy?"

"I want to see!" the other girl said, running over to her sister. They marveled at the flowers and pleaded to their parents to take them to the Grove. Before they left the cabin, the mother turned back to Denny and mouthed "Thank you." Denny nodded and returned the smile before going to his desk and sitting down in his chair. Before he spun around to face forward, someone else came through the door of the cabin.

"Welcome to Redwood National—"

"You can skip the introduction."

The voice was hard, formal, accusatory. What had Denny done now? Did he forget to change the paper towel rolls in the bathrooms? It wasn't even his turn to do that!

Denny oriented himself to the voice and saw a man standing before him. He was dressed in a tan ranger uniform like Denny's, but he had a big badge on the left side of his chest that was absent on Denny's. The man's hands were pocketed and his face was glum. Something had happened; Denny just hoped it wasn't his fault.

"I'm chief ranger Hank Nell," the man said. "Are you the only ranger on duty today?"

Holy shit, Denny thought. "I'm sorry, did you say—"

"Listen, son, I don't have time for this. I'd rather you answer my question and give me some information than gawk at me. So, I'll ask again, are you the only ranger on duty today?"

"No, of course not. I'm just working the desk."

"Obviously."

Denny was slightly hurt by Chief Nell's bluntness. This was his idol, his entire motivation to be a park ranger, and he was being short with him. He now understood why people urged him never to meet his heroes. "I'm sorry, but what is this about?"

Chief Nell walked to the door and flicked the lock closed. Denny was about to tell him he couldn't do that, but he realized that he could. He was the chief, after all. Nell sat on the edge of Denny's desk and gave him that same glum look as before. "You're aware that redwood trees are sacred, yes?"

Denny nodded.

"And you're aware that some people are willing to completely disregard this fact for any number of reasons?"

Denny thought back to the stories he heard about this place when it first opened, about Gary Gerschult. He nodded again.

"There have been a number of break-ins over the past few years. The most recent one was in June. We've done our best to mitigate the situation, but nothing we do seems to be enough."

"What do you mean 'break-ins'? Like the teens in the Grove?"

"Worse."

Denny cocked his head, which prompted Nell to roll his eyes. Again, Denny's pride was struck.

"Let's take a walk," said Nell.

They left the cabin and turned down the trail. Denny followed Nell, who seemed to know where he was going. There was a point when Nell stopped, looked around, and then kept walking. Denny did the same, but saw nothing, no distinguishing factors around them to clue him in on where they were. But Chief Nell continued on, Denny blaming his lack of navigation skills on his inexperience.

"Sorry, I didn't catch your name," Chief Nell said over his shoulder.

"Oh, uh, Denny."

"How long you been here, Oh Uh Denny?"

"About two months, give or take."

"Summer job, huh? Yeah, I thought that too when I first came here. You'll learn the ropes, and then all the world will give you is a chain."

Denny had no idea what that meant, but he didn't ask for clarification. He was already in a hole with Nell because of his incompetence, and he didn't want to dig himself deeper. He just nodded and followed the chief ranger further into the forest. By this point, they were no longer on the trail and all sense of familiarity Denny had was lost.

Finally, Chief Nell stopped walking and stood next to a tree. He pointed to a bare spot on the tree. It didn't look natural. "See this?" Nell asked. "This is what they're after."

"The tree?"

"Not exactly. You know the Giantess?"

"Yeah."

"You know that burl at her base?"

"The huh?"

Nell shook his head. "That weird growth. That's called the Gerschult burl. Surely you know about him, right?"

"Totally."

"People are coming into the park after hours and cutting burls off of trees."

"Why?"

"Burl wood is beautiful, used in ornate pieces. Obviously, those pieces are manufactured from wood that isn't protected under environmental law. This, however, is terrible on so many levels." Chief Nell stood up. "A burl is a tree's way of protecting a weak point, and cutting that burl off only endangers the tree more."

This was all news to Denny. He couldn't understand why someone would even want those weird lumps on trees or how they could be in any way valuable to anyone. "But why would they do this? Why go through all the trouble?"

Nell held up his hand and rubbed the tip of his thumb over the tips of his index and middle finger. "Money," he said. "The more illegal, the more beautiful, the more people are willing to pay to have it in their home."

"How have they not been caught yet?"

"There's almost two hundred square miles to this park, and we are two of twenty rangers on rotating shifts. If you want to walk the entire forest in the dead of night, be my guest. Instead of doing that, I would like you to accompany me with monthly checks, surveying all the trees with burls in a mile radius of the park's main entrance." Nell stepped away from the tree, walking past Denny back toward the trail. "We may have to switch our methods around, depending on how often this keeps happening..."

Instead of following or listening to the chief ranger, Denny looked at the spot on the tree where the burl had been. Looking at the bare wood without bark, he felt the need to protect it—as if he, a five-foot-ten man, could protect it, a three-hundred-foot-tall spire of nature.

Denny craned his neck to look up, trying to see the tree's top, but he couldn't. It was truly breathtaking, being surrounded by these stagnant beasts that weighed more than buildings, towering over him like gods. Denny exhaled and it felt like his soul had left his body. He finally found the strength to peel himself away from the overwhelming grasp of nature and saw Chief Nell, looking at him and smiling.

"What?" Denny asked.

"I know that look, Oh Uh Denny," Nell replied. "You've only known patty cake your whole life, and you've just been introduced to hopscotch."

Denny didn't know how to feel about the fact that he somewhat understood that one.

5

NINE MONTHS BEFORE

Sam's senior year of high school began with stares and whispers. While he approached his new locker, which took him a bit too long to find, people turned from their circles of conversation to sneak a peek at him, then go back and recite one of the many rumors that had circulated throughout the class over the summer. While he tried and failed to input his combination for the third time, Sam thought he heard someone say that he had to get bailed out of jail for what he did to Cory, which was an outright dumb rumor since all Sam did was splash some beer in Cory's face. If anything, Cory should've been the one in jail.

Sam was unsure if this new notoriety was entirely bad; last year, people couldn't care less about him, and now he was the talk of the school. When he finally got his locker open and deposited his backpack inside it, he decided that he would play into the gossip if asked about it. But it turned out that even though Sam and Cory's fight was the hottest topic, no one wanted anything to do with the story's perpetrator.

Until the day before Thanksgiving break, when Sam was pulled out of math class to go to the school counselor's office.

He walked in there confused and Ms. Baker swiveled in her chair to greet him. Sam sat in the chair on the other side of her desk and waited impatiently as she clacked away on her keyboard. There was a jar of unlabeled, individually-wrapped candies on the desk, discs of multiple flavors and colors. Ms. Baker squinted her eyes at the computer screen and then leaned back in her chair. "So," she said, "how are you?"

Sam furrowed his brow. "What do you mean?"

"How are you doing?"

"I'm... fine?"

"Why is that a question?"

"Why are you asking me how I am?"

"Because it's my job to care about you and, looking at what's happened over the past few months, I feel like there's some work to be done."

Sam inhaled, trying to keep all the words in his head. It was her job to care about him? The woman he'd seen four times in his entire high school career was supposed to care about him? Who was she kidding? She had the entire student body to worry about—why would she give a shit about someone like Sam? "Alright," was all he said.

"Well, don't you agree? Your GPA has taken a rather scary dive from last year. You've dropped a whole half-point in three months."

Whole half-point? How could I even try take this seriously? "Yeah, things have been difficult for me ever since my dad died."

Ms. Baker clicked her mouse a few times. "You raised your grade by two letters mere weeks after your father's death, and now, months after, your grades have tanked. I find it hard to believe that grief is the reason for that."

Sam shrugged. "It's different for everybody."

"Look Sam, I'm not going to sugar coat this. If you keep performing like this, you're never going to graduate."

"Who said I wanted to?"

"You did. In your freshman year."

"What are you talking about?"

Ms. Baker clicked a few more times and typed something, then clicked once more and spun her monitor around so Sam could see. "Does this look familiar to you?"

It did. "My future goals sheet."

"And what does that say there after the question, 'What would you most like to accomplish?'"

"'I want to graduate high school at the top of my class.' I had high hopes."

"You had big dreams."

"I had stupid dreams. There was no way I was ever going to be valedictorian."

Ms. Baker pursed her lips. "But there was a way. All you had to do was—"

"I swear, if you're about to tell me I should've applied myself, I'm leaving."

The counselor smirked at Sam. "See? You are smart after all."

Sam groaned and stood up from the chair. He started to leave, then backpedaled and dug his hand into the jar of candy on Ms. Baker's desk. He pulled out a green one and took the wrapper off.

"Just think about it, Sam. I know you can do it."

Sam popped the candy into his mouth and left the room, heading back to his math class to do absolutely nothing.

The car pulled into the driveway fifteen minutes after it was supposed to. It wasn't the worst thing that could've happened; they could have arrived a half hour early and the table wouldn't have be done, then Darren would have to chew Cherry out to appeal to the buyer, and then the deal would be off to an awkward start. Luckily, that didn't happen, and Cherry was able to put the finishing touches on the table before the buyer arrived.

"They're running late," Darren said, walking into the shop. Cherry was rubbing a polishing cloth on the wooden surface. "Looks good."

"Thanks," said Cherry. He shook a hand through his red hair, sawdust showering from his scalp and to the floor. "Help me bring it out?"

Darren nodded and put on a pair of gloves before handling the table. The two of them hoisted it up and carried it out the garage door, walking it to the front of the house. Darren was mesmerized by the patterns in the wood, swirls of red and orange following the flow of the grain. It reminded him of the flow of deep red following the slope of the hill, trickling down, seeping into the dirt, dyeing the green grass a hot, dark color.

"Admiring my handiwork?" Cherry asked as they set the table down on the ground.

Darren grunted as he stood up, his back cracking and eyes peeling away from the table, out of his memory. "Yeah. I think we could negotiate high for this one."

The buyer got out of his car as Vic came out of the house. The four of them met around the table in the driveway, standing on opposite sides. If the table wasn't below knee height, they might have done business over it.

"It's beautiful," the buyer said. He crouched down to inspect it, running a finger around the bark on the edge of the table. "This is real?"

"Pure," Vic said. "Hauled it myself." Darren had to keep himself from blurting out that Vic had the easiest job of the three of them.

"Very fine craftsmanship, gentlemen."

"Thank you," said Darren. "We just finished up on it."

"I can tell," their buyer said, inhaling deeply. "I can still smell the polish." He stood and smiled. "So, price."

"Right," Cherry said. He took out his phone and began reading from it. "When you first contacted us, you asked for a circular coffee table with a diameter of three feet on black stainless-steel legs. You agreed to a base price of seven grand and were aware that the price could fluctuate depending on wood quality and prep time."

The buyer chuckled. "So, what's the damage?"

"Fourteen," Cherry said bluntly.

"Hundred?"

Cherry shook his head.

"Thousand? The price doubled?" The buyer laughed again, this time for a lot longer and more genuinely than the last. "Yeah guys, I really don't know."

"You gave us three days after we got the burl to turn it into a coffee table. If it weren't illegal wood, I'd tell you to go ask anyone if what we did should be possible, and they'd all say no."

"See, that's what I'm worried about. What if it's all prettied up, you know, made to look like redwood, but it's some cheap shit I could order online?"

Darren twitched. Was this guy really questioning them? "We assure you it's redwood. How else could we get that color?"

The buyer knelt down and looked closely at the table. "Paint?"

"Why go through the trouble of replication when you could go for the real thing?"

"So you could rip off people for thousands of dollars."

Darren bit his cheek. "Take a deeper whiff. Try to smell the wood over the polish."

As the buyer put his nose close to the table and inhaled, Darren put his hand on the back of the buyer's head and slammed his face into the wood. Blood sprayed and the buyer wailed, covered his nose and backed away from the table. "What the fuck? What is wrong with you?"

Darren rounded the table and got in the buyer's face. "You think you know better than me? I made this shit, okay? We cut this shit in the middle of the night for you! I made this for you!"

"You sick fuck!" He spat blood in Darren's face. "Do you think I'm going to pay you now? You're done!"

"If you go to anyone, especially the cops, you're in far more trouble than I am."

The buyer looked up at Darren, lips quivering and eyes tearing up, filled with confusion.

"You didn't hear me. I made this *for you*. You came to me, fully knowing that the table would be illegal. You employed me to make this, to *steal* this wood!"

"I did not!"

Darren rapped his hand repeatedly on the table. "This was all you, man! This was all you!"

"Stop!"

Darren stopped, the pounding ceasing. The buyer's blood was smeared across his hand, splashed all over the table.

"I'll take it," the buyer said. "Fourteen thousand. Fine."

"Good," Darren said, "because if you didn't, your head would've replaced my hand smacking that table." He stood up, knowing that his threat was clunky at best, but he didn't care. The buyer was already unfolding hundred dollar bills out of his pocket, and Darren was more than happy to take them off his hands.

6

Six Months Before

When temperatures dipped into the mid-to-high forties and low fifties, people became reluctant to go outside. Not just because of the conditions; half of the population of California was still hungover from their New Year's Eve ragers, and plenty more just didn't feel like being productive. Denny was the exception—the working bit, not the drunk bit. He and Chief Nell sat in the ranger's cabin together while rain poured outside, washed down the windows, pooled up in potholes. Nell was talking Denny's ear off while Denny did his best not to hurl all over the desk.

"It's a real mean one out there, huh?" Chief Nell said, standing at the window.

Denny offered a grunt as agreement.

"I don't mind the rain, really. I don't remember the last time we got something this big. It's just a matter of driving in it, you know? One second you're fine, and the next you're hydroplaning all over the place." The chief ranger turned around and saw Denny slumped at the desk, head propped up on one hand. "Why did you even come in today? Look at that, you're drooling on yourself!"

Denny glowered and wiped his hand on his pants. "Someone's gotta man the desk," he said.

"Not today. Trails are closed because of the rain. Can't have any tourists getting swept away by mudslides."

"Why are we here, then?"

Chief Nell grinned. "No tourists means no one to ask us questions, no one to have to help out when their kids are unruly, no one to keep track of to make sure they're not out rolling in the redwoods."

Denny wasn't sure if his lack of understanding was because of his inebriation or because of the chief's insistence on using the batshit craziest expressions he'd ever heard. "Can you run that by me again," Denny asked, "this time without all the old man lingo?"

"No tourists means you and I are going to take a look at the burls out there." He walked past Denny and down the hallway to the supply room.

"What? No, no way!"

"We have to do our monthly checks, like we agreed upon! Today's the day." There was rustling from the supply closet, followed by the chief saying "Where the hell are they?"

"Why don't we wait for a day with better conditions?"

"The longer we wait, the more time the thieves will have to steal what isn't theirs."

Denny groaned as Chief Nell emerged from the supply closet holding a plastic package in each hand. "What are those?"

"Ponchos," Nell replied. "Gotta stay dry somehow, right?" He set one of the packages on the desk in front of Denny.

"Yeah. But, hey, what about those mudslides? I don't think the ponchos will protect us against those."

"Didn't you hear me, Oh Uh Denny? *Tourists* can't get swept up in mudslides, but *we* are not tourists. We're..." He looked at Denny with big eyes, expecting him to finish his sentence. "Come on, what are we?"

Denny sighed and ripped open his package. "We're rangers." Which apparently meant they were expendable when it came to natural disasters.

Chief Nell led Denny into the forest, raindrops pelting their ponchos. Denny was surprised at how well they were holding up; the only thing that was really getting wet were his boots, which he thanked his past self for wearing. He couldn't imagine being out here in sneakers.

"Son of a bitch!" Chief Nell shouted as he approached a tree. Denny didn't even need to ask what it was about. He was able to find what they were looking for a lot quicker after these surveys. Nell elected for them to go out more frequently for some time, but after they found nothing out of the ordinary for three searches in a row, they went back to their monthly schedule. Not only could Denny tell that there was a burl missing, but also that Chief Nell was cursing himself for not making weekly searches the default. "They got another one!"

"How long ago?"

Nell shook his head. "Not sure. You can't really tell how long it's been, but given that there's no sawdust anywhere, no splinters sticking off the tree where it was cut, it was probably a while ago."

"Not necessarily," said Denny. "I mean, couldn't the rain have washed it all away?"

The chief mulled Denny's suggestion over for a moment. "I suppose it could have. But still, they cut another burl."

Denny allowed himself to feel a little bit of pride for thinking of something Nell hadn't. He was constantly learning new things on this job; flower names, harmful shrubbery, which plants' leaves you could wipe your butt with and not get a horrible rash. But still, it always seemed that Nell knew more than Denny could ever find out. It wasn't every day he outsmarted the man—in fact, this was the first time in recent memory that it happened at all.

"Let's head back to the cabin," said Chief Nell, defeated. "Try not to slip and die on our way back."

"Chief," Denny said, "we should really call someone about this, you know?"

"I'm not sure I do."

"Like, don't you think the cops would be able to help us track these guys down?"

Chief Nell laughed and turned to Denny. "Kid, we are the cops. The police are too worried about murderers and meth heads to care about trees."

As the chief turned away and continued walking back to the cabin, Denny felt his pride slip away with the rain slicking off his poncho.

When the two reached the edge of the woods, they saw a truck parked in the lot. The running boards were nearly falling off, and the exterior was the same orange color as the rust that plagued the truck. Its wear and tear was hard to notice, aside from the smudged windows and broken hubcaps.

The chief looked at Denny, confused. "Is that piece of shit yours?"

Denny shook his head and turned to the cabin. He saw a man standing in front of the door, tilting his head and trying to peer inside. The man started to round the corner for the window, but stopped when he saw Denny and Nell walking up to him. "Hey, rangers," he said. "Mighty storm that blew in, huh?"

Chief Nell just stood and stared at the man, not saying anything. Denny gave the chief a sideways glance before he stepped in to say something. "Yeah, real bad out here," he said. "We're sorry, sir, but the trails are closed today. It's our number-one priority to keep hikers safe, and I'm afraid we can't do that in these conditions."

The man shook his head. "No, I totally understand. I'll come back another day. Thank you." He stepped off the cabin's wooden porch and made for the truck in the parking lot, splashing through rainwater on his way. Denny walked up to the cabin door and unlocked it before taking off his poncho and shaking it out under the canopy. The chief, however, stood in the rain and watched the truck drive away.

"Hey, chief!" Denny yelled. "What are you doing?" Instead of answering, Chief Nell turned around and walked silently into the cabin, not bothering to take off his poncho. He brushed past Denny and some of the water on the poncho soaked into Denny's shirt. "Chief, what the hell?"

"Shut it," said Nell, "I need to think."

"About what? What's going on?"

Chief Nell finally took off his poncho and hung it on a coat rack in the corner to dry. He sat behind the desk and kicked up his feet, caressing his chin while he stared into space and thought.

"Chief? Chief, what is it?" Still, he didn't answer. Denny crossed into the chief's line of sight, got right up in his face. "Hank! What the hell is going on?"

"Jesus, Denny, would you let me think?"

"Was it the guy in the parking lot?"

Chief Nell sighed, threw up his hands in disgust, and answered Denny. "Yes, it was the guy in the parking lot. He reminded me of something."

"What?"

"When did you start here?"

"Uh... June, I think?"

"Then you should've heard about this, at least in passing from one of the other rangers. Someone was killed here back in May. I went out into the woods with two other rangers and, when we found them, things got real ugly real fast."

"What happened?"

"Shootout."

Chief Nell said it so casually, but Denny was blown away. "What? Why would there be a shootout in the park? I thought weapons were banned here."

"Signs don't do anything against people who don't care. One of them pulled a gun and aimed it at us, so we had no choice but to fire back. I shot and killed one, and someone else injured the other."

"Who was it? Who was it that died, I mean."

The chief shrugged. "Pretty sure they were both locals, so at least the legal side of it was easy. We called the families, let them know what happened, but I don't remember a name. But that guy we just saw? I swear he was there that day."

Denny felt his face go slack. Hank had shot and killed somebody? He couldn't imagine it. Well, he could, but he didn't like to. Had Denny ever walked past the place it happened while he was on patrol? He must have—there was always that one spot where he seemed to get the chills for no reason, even in sweltering heat. That had to be where it went down.

"So, you think that guy was the one they injured?" Denny asked.

"No," Chief Nell said. "I think he was the one I killed."

Trails at Redwood National Park opened up three days later. While Denny and the chief were out checking the burl locations, they also made sure to test the walkways, step down the paths some so people wouldn't get lost on the washed-away trails. They determined that ground was sturdy enough for tourists and that no burls had been taken, which came as no surprise to Denny. Chief Nell, on the other hand, was skeptical about the whole situation. "They're probably taking the ones we're not monitoring," he told Denny the morning trails opened up. "Maybe we need to expand our perimeter."

"Or," Denny said, "they're not taking any burls, and we're all good."

The chief pursed his lips, shook his head, curled his tongue in his mouth so he didn't lash out against Denny. Let that happen to some poor, unsuspecting tourist who asked a bad question to the wrong ranger.

Denny once again worked the front desk, helping people find their way around the park, answering any questions they might have. He just finished up helping a woman find the Giantess—"It's right on the sign outside, ma'am."—when Ranger Vanessa came through the door with a tour group in tow.

"And here we have our amazing ranger cabin, where one of the park's twenty rangers are stationed to help all of you!" Vanessa said cheerfully. "Right now, Ranger Denny is manning the desk. Feel free to ask him any questions you can think of!"

People began talking over each other, rapid-firing at Denny. He made eye contact with Vanessa and she flashed a smile and sent a wink his way. That made his heart flutter; she started working at the park in December, and ever since then, Denny was infatuated with her. They became close work friends, planning their shifts and coordinating their breaks to spend more time together. One time after one of those shared shifts, Vanessa had asked Denny if he wanted to go get drinks, but he turned her down for some stupid reason. He hated himself ever since.

"How tall are the trees?" asked a young boy toward the front of the group.

Denny gathered himself, tearing his eyes away from Vanessa and giving his attention to the groups' questions. "Well, most of the redwood trees in the park are over two hundred feet tall. But we have a few that are taller than two-fifty, and the Giantess is the tallest tree in the park at three hundred-sixty feet!"

The same little boy raised his hand and didn't wait to be called on to ask his next question. "Is that bigger than an airplane?"

Denny laughed, as did most of the people in the tour group. "Yes, much bigger." He scanned the group for another raised hand and called on a woman wearing a bright blue puff jacket. "What's your question?"

"Does the cold climate affect the trees at all?" she asked.

"Well, California is part of a warmer climate region, and that's what redwood trees like. I mean, think of the Midwest—for them it's probably well below freezing, but we here barely need to bundle up."

"Speak for yourself," the woman said. "I'm wearing this, and I'm still chilly!"

Denny pointed to a man at the right of the group, standing next to Vanessa. After he put his hand down, he combed his fingers through his red hair a few times before asking his question. "How many burls would you say are in the park?"

"I'm sorry?" Denny asked.

"Burls, you know. The growths on the trees."

"Yeah, of course. Umm..." He was stammering, but he wasn't sure if it was from his fear of seeming dumb in front of Vanessa or because of the man's question. Did he really just ask about burls? Was this the thief? "I don't have an exact number, but burls are very common on trees. Especially here, with the droughts that often happen in the summertime, forest fires can damage the trees and they'll form burls to cover that damage up." Denny glanced quickly at Vanessa and she nodded her head at him. *Nice*, Denny thought. *She doesn't think I'm a total idiot.*

"What about the Gerschult burl?" the same man asked again.

"What about it?"

"How big is it?"

Denny scrunched his face in thought, dug through his memory to try and find statistics for the burl. It added a fair amount of volume onto the base of the Giantess, but how much exactly? And why did this guy even care? Just as Denny was about to give up, say that he didn't know for sure, the door opened behind the tour group, which quickly parted to let whoever came in through.

"Ah, I see we've got a tour going on!" Chief Nell said as he made his way to the front of the group. "Have they been behaving, Ranger Vanessa?"

"Oh, they sure have," she replied, giving the chief a thumbs-up.

"That guy over there says that the trees are bigger than airplanes!" the little boy piped up, pointing at Denny across the room.

Chief Nell looked over at the desk ranger and smirked. "Well, he sure knows a lot about the trees, doesn't he?" Nell said to the boy. He walked over to Denny and stood at the corner of the desk.

"Someone asked a question about the Gerschult burl before you came in," Denny said to the chief. "Maybe you could shed some light on that topic, and answer some more questions while I talk to Ranger Vanessa outside for a minute?"

Chief Nell squinted his eyes, shifted them back and forth. Denny could tell he understood the signal; the man was all for catching these burl thieves, and even though the redhead might not know or care about the trees at all, Denny couldn't help but wonder if he had something to do with the poaching. Chief Nell nodded, spun around to face the group, and said, "Of course, Ranger Denny! Come on, folks. Hit me with your best shot!"

While people raised their hands and pleaded to be called upon by the chief ranger, Denny nudged through the crowd and motioned for Vanessa to follow him. They stood on the cabin's porch while they talked.

"What's up?" asked Vanessa.

"Not much," Denny replied. "How much longer is your tour?"

She checked her watch. "About fifteen minutes. Why? You wanna go on break after?" She gave him a smile and batted her eyes.

"Heh, maybe. But could you maybe keep tabs on the redhead guy? The one who asked about the Gerschult burl?"

Vanessa's flirtatious demeanor disappeared as quickly as it came on. "Uh, I suppose. How come?"

Denny looked around them to see if anyone was listening in on their conversation. "I think he might have something to do with the burl poaching," he said in a hushed tone.

"Poaching? Like what the chief is worried about?"

Denny nodded.

"Sure, I guess," Vanessa said, unsure of herself.

"Thank you. Just keep an eye on him, you know? Make sure he's not straying from the trails. And if he asks more shifty questions, let me know."

"Will do." Vanessa walked to the door and held it open for Denny to go through before her. He squeezed once again through the tour group while Vanessa remained near the back. "Alright, folks," she said to the group, "we only have time for one more question for Chief Nell before we have to start moving again."

Chief Nell called on the woman in the blue puff jacket. "Do you guys have boots to rent?" she asked. "My feet are killing me, and it's so cold out there!" Denny looked down at the woman's feet and noticed she was wearing a pair of thin sneakers.

The chief scoffed. "No, we don't rent out shoes. What do we look like, a bowling alley?"

There it is, Denny thought. *Let him lash out at someone else.*

7

Five Months Before

Sam opened the back door of his house and was met with the most terrifying sight he could think of: his mother standing apprehensively at the kitchen table.

His mind raced with all the things he'd done wrong recently, flashes of mischief running through his head. Was it the skipping? He hadn't skipped class since after winter break—he wasn't quite ready for it to end, plus they came back to school on a Thursday. Sam didn't think it was worth it to come in for two days of the week, so he took those days to himself. Maybe his mother found the vodka bottle under his bed. But if she had, it would be sitting on the table next to her, and she would gesture to it with big eyes that said "What the hell is this?" and then Sam would stammer about how it wasn't his until his mom would shut him up and ground him or something. This time, though, all that was sitting on the table was his mother's phone, open to a screen he couldn't quite see.

"Hello," Sam said, stepping into the house and closing the door.

His mother gestured at her phone with big eyes. "Care to explain?" she asked.

"What's going on?" He approached the table and looked at the phone. The display showed a black screen with a table of numbers he'd never seen before. Sam was smart enough to know it was her banking app, but not smart enough to figure out what exactly his mother was accusing him of. "Explain what?" Sam asked. "What is this?"

"This is my credit card statement for last month," she said. "Do you notice anything odd about it? Or maybe familiar?"

Sam looked over every number on the screen, every date and location the card was used, and found nothing out of the sort. Then again, he didn't really know what he was looking for. "I mean, there's the grocery store we go to," he said, pointing to one of the cells in the table. He moved his finger down to the cell underneath. "That's the hair salon, right? You got a haircut last month."

His mother scrolled a little bit to the bottom of the table, showing her most recent credit card transactions. She pointed to the third cell from the bottom. "How about that one? That's an ATM withdrawal made last week. Two hundred dollars."

"Okay..."

"I didn't withdraw anything, Sam! I would never use my credit card at an ATM!"

"Are you saying I did? How would I even do that?"

"Come on, Sam! Don't play dumb with me. It's so easy to just take my card from my wallet, and I know you've done it before!"

Sam couldn't deny that it was super easy to take his mom's credit card, but he only did it in emergency situations—when he had no cash or needed to get food after school. But, like skipping class, he hadn't taken it in a while, even before winter break. His Christmas shopping list went down exponentially since he had no friends, and he bought the gift for his mom with his own money. He was nice enough to do that. "I didn't do this, mom," Sam said.

"Sure you didn't," she replied, shaking her head. "Whatever. If you don't want to fess up, I'll just ground you."

"Great, what else is new?" Sam walked away from the kitchen, heading toward his room. His mom was quiet for a few seconds, then dropped a bomb:

"I'll also just stop giving you cash whenever you ask for it. Since you obviously didn't care enough to ask this time."

That made Sam pause. He hoped it didn't show, but he was shaking at the thought of being cut off. Since his father died, his mom gave him a break when it came to getting a job. She figured it would help lessen the stress and let him focus more on school, but his grades were showing that it wasn't the case. Now he would have to find something, and fast. Because despite what his mom thought, Sam was telling the truth: he was not the one to make that withdrawal.

He was in the clouds, far away from everything and everyone. He took a deep breath that tasted like his childhood, good and sweet and pure. He almost didn't want to exhale it. Instead, Darren held it in and savored the breath, which only sent him higher into the air. He was like a balloon.

Eventually he was high enough to reach the stars. Although it was cold, they radiated with such intensity that Darren didn't notice the chilly bite of space. He felt as if he was curled up in a blanket, swaddled like a baby. Still, he did not breathe.

The stars began to talk to him, whispers at first. They blended together in a mess of what sounded like wind rustling through a forest in the middle of fall. The middle of fall. The middle of the forest. The middle of his chest. The blood poured from the middle of his chest and trickled down his shirt, stained it red, horrible red. He choked on it, rusty spit dripped from the corner of his mouth. Darren watched, unable to move, feeling caught, encroached, surrounded, about to die.

"Help me."

He couldn't.

A sharp pain in his shoulder sent him to the ground.

"Darren!"

He jumped up from the cushy recliner, letting out a well-supported scream and followed it up by hyperventilating. Darren's vision was foggy, nose runny, mouth void of any moisture. His tongue felt like sandpaper against his teeth. He swallowed nothing, then chewed on the inside of his cheek, an old trick he'd learned to speed up salivation. Vic was looking at him, one of his hands on Darren's shoulder. "You good, man?"

Darren nodded as if nothing had been wrong.

"You were holding your breath for so long, man. We thought you were going to pass out."

"Was I not passed out already?"

Vic shook his head. "You were just staring into space."

"Huh. I was just zoning out, I think," Darren lied. "No big deal."

It was in fact a big deal. This was the first he'd thought about it in months, and the fact that it happened during a trip was all the more telling of what the cause was. Darren took notice of the glass pipe in his hand, the lighter on the floor, and the small plastic baggie dusted with rock powder on the side table next to him.

"You took a big hit," said Cherry from across the room. "Maybe you should quit for a while."

Darren turned his head slowly to face him. "No, I gotta do more. Go bigger. We need to go bigger." He reached for the baggie and rubbed his finger around inside it, the powder clinging to his clammy skin. He inserted the tip of his finger into his nose and snorted deeply. Darren felt the powder in his sinuses and stifled a cough, then a sneeze. He couldn't look like a pussy in front of these guys. "We gotta go bigger," he said again.

"What do you mean?" Vic asked. "We don't have any more, you just snorted the rest."

"That's not what I mean, you fucking moron."

Vic recoiled from the insult. "Whoa, asshole!"

"Shut up." Darren pointed at Vic—or at least tried to. There were multiple of him, so he just picked out the one that looked the most real. "We need to start cutting more hunks off the trees."

"Burls," Cherry said. "They're called burls."

"I don't give a shit what they're called! We need more of them! We need more cash!"

"Who would even want to buy from us anymore, Darren?" Vic asked. "You broke one of our only buyers' noses!"

"That was months ago! He's forgotten about that by now! We're probably getting recommended all across the state for our craftsmanship!"

"I'm not so sure," Cherry said. "I think what we need to do is call Robbie and—"

Darren clutched his pipe and hucked it at Cherry's head. It missed and shattered against the basement wall, but Cherry still made a big fuss. "What the fuck, Darren!"

"Don't ever say that name! Don't mention him, don't even think about him! Fuck you for saying that, fuck you! And you made me break my pipe, good fucking job!"

Darren started hyperventilating again, beads of sweat beginning to form and collect and run down his face. Vic and Cherry just stared at him while his chest heaved, air hissing through Darren's gritted teeth. He stopped to lick his lips, his eye twitching as he ran his tongue across the chapped skin. His blinking became rapid, his breath beginning to slow. He was losing it. If he didn't snap himself out of it, he'd go back there, see him bleeding, dying, calling for help he'd never get. Darren coughed, brought himself back to reality, and looked at Vic and Cherry. "We gotta go big," he said.

"It's gonna take a lot of planning, Darren," Vic said. "And probably more people than just us."

"He's right," agreed Cherry. "I saw it, and it's huge. There's no way we can get it out of there by ourselves."

Darren shook his head. "I don't care. Whatever needs to be done, get it done. I want it."

They all exchanged looks, ones of worry, confusion, determination, or mixtures of the three. Darren could see the fear on their faces. They looked pathetic, like little kids scared of the monster in the closet. Vic showed it more than Cherry. What was Vic even afraid of? All he had to do was drive them the hell away when the job was done. Darren and Cherry—and apparently some others—would be the ones actually doing the work out there, lugging the thing back to the truck, all while dodging whatever the rangers threw at them.

Was it going to be a hard job? Yes, probably the hardest one they've ever done. But did that mean it was impossible? Not at fucking all.

Cherry was the one who said what Darren wanted to hear. "Alright. One more, and then the big one."

Darren smiled. "Good. I want that big chunk of wood."

"Burl," Cherry corrected. "It's called a burl."

8

Three Months Before

Sam's head rattled against the bus window, the buzz of the vehicle and the sound of his scalp hitting the glass drowning out the childish squeals of his classmates. Who thought it was a good idea to send the seniors on a field trip? Sure, it was a good idea to get everyone in the class together before graduation, but a field trip? Hadn't they outgrown those? Sam thought so, until two weeks ago when a class-wide email was sent out, advertising a final trip for them to Redwood National Park. It was optional, but everyone was encouraged to go and spend time out in nature with the people they'd grown up with.

At first, Sam had no intention of partaking in the trip; he'd much rather just have the day off. But after giving it some more thought, he realized he would have little to do, with his grounding still being in effect. He'd be confined to the house, but couldn't watch TV or play video games, couldn't have friends over. He wasn't even sure if his mother was going to be home, so he would be alone, fending for himself against monotonous insanity.

Sam decided not to take the chance of going crazy and signed up for the trip. After all, just because no one cared about him didn't mean he didn't care about them. That was the case for the majority of the class, but there was still a place for Bradley in Sam's mind. They had warmed up to each other recently, not really having full conversations but at the very least nodding to each other when they passed in the halls. It was a rather small step toward friendship for span of almost a year, but a step nonetheless.

Bradley's presence on the trip was one of the two reasons Sam wanted to go on the field trip. The other reason was that Mr. Veranda, his junior year biology teacher, was one of the chaperones. It made sense for him to be there when Sam remembered all the time they spent on trees in the class—it wouldn't have surprised Sam at all if Mr. Veranda had been the one to suggest the park as the field trip destination.

The teens in the bus rumbled more and more as they neared the park, the trees lining the road getting taller and taller. Sam's classmates gawked at their height, towering over everything like the skyscrapers in the city. Sam had no choice but to look out the window at them, as his forehead was still pressed against the glass and bounced whenever the bus did. His sight of the trees was shaky, as if there was an earthquake and the whole world was trembling. He gave his head a rest and separated it from the window to get a clear look at the forest. Although he didn't care about much of anything, much less about a bunch of trees, Sam had to admit they were quite the thing to witness. He's always heard stories of people coming to California just to see the redwoods—"Oh, it's been my dream since I was little."—and refused to believe that anyone would travel here for something they could see online, in textbooks, and not spend so much money on. Lucky for Sam, it only cost him his dignity, which he lost the second he climbed onto that bright yellow school bus for the first time since sophomore year.

He felt better once he stepped off the dingy bus onto the gravel that made up the parking lot. No amount of open windows could take away the reek of old vomit that lingered in the cushy seats, but being immersed in something—anything—other than that was pleasant by comparison.

Across the parking lot stood a cabin, and standing on the cabin's porch were two people, a man and a woman, dressed in beige clothing. The guy waved to the group of oncoming teenagers, which Sam thought was a bit much. Did he really need to look so ecstatic? The sun was beating down on them, and they were all about to spend who knows how long traipsing through the wilderness. This guy would be sweating through his khaki pants in no time.

When the group got close enough to the cabin, Sam realized that the rangers before them looked about as old as he was. Neither of them could possibly be over twenty-five, and he was heavily questioning whether the guy ranger could even drink legally. Why were they letting practical children work here? Were those *guns* on their utility belts?

"Hey, everyone!" the guy ranger said. "I'm Ranger Denny, this is Ranger Vanessa, and we are so happy to have you here at Redwood National Park! You guys picked a pretty warm day to swing by, but if there's one thing we Californians can handle, it's the heat!"

Ranger Denny paused, probably for whoops of agreement, but none came from the sea of nearly a hundred high schoolers. He continued on, his spiel sounding a lot more disappointed than Sam thought it should be.

"Okay, well, you guys are a pretty large group here today. We normally have a cap of fifteen people to a tour group, but we're more than happy to make an exception. Obviously, I can't keep track of all you by myself, so we're going to be splitting you guys in half. One group will be led by me, and the other group will be led by Ranger Vanessa."

"I hope I get the chick," a boy next to Sam whispered to his friend. "Look at her tits!" The two boys held back laughter as Sam rolled his eyes. *If they do get to be in a group with her, that'll be the closest either of them will ever get to a woman,* he thought.

Ranger Denny held out an arm and pretended to slice the group down the middle. People instinctively moved to one side or the other, those left standing in the open space stepping quickly to the side most of their friends were on.

"Perfect!" Ranger Denny said. He pointed at the side Sam was on. "This group is with me!" The two boys that commented on Ranger Vanessa's physique groaned in defeat, prompting Sam to roll his eyes at them again. Ranger Denny took a few steps on the porch to the approximate middle of his tour group. "Okay guys, just so we're not in the way of Ranger Vanessa's group, we're going to start off by heading to the Ring. If you'll just follow me back behind the ranger cabin to the trail, we'll get started!"

Ranger Denny hopped off the porch and disappeared from Sam's sight. The people in front of him started filing forward slowly, talking with each other about how pretty the trees were. Sam glanced around, mostly unimpressed. He'd seen trees before—what was so special about these?

As if he read Sam's mind, Mr. Veranda came up beside him and said, "You know, redwood trees are integral to the forest's ecosystem. Without them, the landscape would be completely different and wouldn't thrive as much as it does."

"Oh wow, I didn't know that," Sam said. He began looking around for anyone else to talk to.

"Well, you must have forgotten what you learned in my class last year."

"Yeah, I guess I did." Sam said it without thinking, but didn't much care about Mr. Veranda's reaction to his absent-minded response. What he really cared about was Bradley and whether they were in the same tour group. He searched in the crowd, scanning every face, stopping in one spot and letting bodies flow past him like a rock in a stream. After a few seconds of waiting, Sam spotted Bradley at the very back of the group and a wave of relief rushed over him. He didn't want to talk to him now, of course, but he'd wait until the tour was well underway to make himself known. That way, he wouldn't make the situation awkward from the get-go, which he knew it would be otherwise.

"Not all the trees in Redwood National Park are redwoods," said Ranger Denny as he walked the group along the trail. "That would be almost impossible by natural standards. Besides, the redwood trees are necessary for everything else in the forest to thrive." Sam saw Mr. Veranda nodding his head after everything Ranger Denny said.

The forest cover became thicker the further they trekked. At one point, the sun was mostly blocked out and the tour group was walking under complete shadow. Eventually, the light returned little by little, and Denny was sure to explain why. "The forest canopy is thicker in some places than others. Did you notice that there wasn't a whole lot of ground vegetation in the darker areas? That's because it's almost impossible for them to survive with little to no sunlight."

Sam wondered if Ranger Denny went through the same speech with every group. It must be curated for a younger or less educated audience, because everything Denny was saying was incredibly obvious. Sam stopped paying attention to the speeches after the third or fourth time Ranger Denny displayed his possession of common sense, which some of the kids in Sam's class seemed to be lacking; they were oohing and ahhing at Denny's fun facts.

How are these kids graduating? Sam thought.

The canopy opened up to the sky, a circle of sunlight projected on the mostly blank forest floor. The circle was surrounded by redwood trees that lined the circle almost perfectly. Sam shared a moment of awe with the rest of his group as they scanned their eyes up and down the scene before them, everyone craning their necks to try and see the tops of the trees.

Ranger Denny hopped up on a fallen log and spoke out over the group. "Now, I know I said before that perfection is almost impossible in nature, but this is one of those cases where nature got really, really close. Welcome to the Ring!"

This time when Denny paused, there was noticeable chatter among the people in the group. The ranger seemed satisfied with himself and continued. "Here we have twenty-six redwood trees taking over a ring of the forest more than a hundred feet in diameter. It truly is a feat of nature. Now, we have about fifteen minutes in this space before we have to move on, so I'll let you guys explore a little. Feel free to take all the pictures you want, and don't stray too far!"

The class slowly dispersed, some stepping into the Ring and becoming showered in sunlight, others staying on the outside and walking around, looking at the trees that formed the Ring. Sam found himself somewhere in between, leaning up against one of the redwood trees and feeling its bark on his back. Of course there were cracks, but the massive proportions of the tree spread them out so they were basically imperceptible through Sam's shirt. He turned around and felt it with the bare skin on his hands, running his fingertips over the tree like a child clawing at their parent's leg to get their attention. He felt a strange connection to this huge tree, this near freak of nature that he'd never felt before for anything. It almost made him cry. He didn't like it.

Sam removed his hand from the tree, looking between it and his hand like the tree had just caused him great pain. And maybe it had.

The air was noticeably warmer in the center of the Ring with all the sun pouring in. It felt better on Sam's skin than the tree bark. He walked alone in the circle of light, trying not to look like a hippie basking in the sunlight and breathing in nature. He kept his arms at his sides, not outstretching them in any way. The longer he lingered, though, the harder it was for him to retain his indifferent composure; he wanted desperately to cast his arms out and twirl around with whimsy. But he didn't, fearing that his classmates would judge, point, and stare like they had at the beginning of the year. He allowed himself to twirl a little, though, disguising it as spinning around in the Ring and looking up at the treetops. It satisfied his whimsy just enough to stop struggling against it.

As he was spinning, Sam bumped into someone and quickly turned around to apologize. But when he saw who it was, he was at a loss for words and began stammering.

"Whoa," Bradley said. "You good?" He spoke without fully recognizing Sam. When he did, his face changed from one of concern to one of confusion. "Oh, hey. What's up?"

"I, uh…" Why was he so nervous? Up until a few weeks ago, Sam had barely seen his old locker neighbor, and he was completely fine with that. Now, his tongue felt numb and his hands on fire. They were sweating and Sam balled them into fists, hoping that would somehow help the clamminess.

"What's this douche doing, Brad?" a boy accompanying Bradley said, stepping past him and closer to Sam. There was something familiar about the boy's face, but Sam didn't realize until Bradley spoke again.

"Nothing, Cory. Step off."

Of course. Tallboy: how could Sam have forgotten that all too punchable face? He wished he had a beer to throw at him, but alcohol was prohibited in the park.

"Oh, I remember this guy," Cory said. He sneered and revealed a row of surprisingly white teeth. "Back for round two, huh?"

Bradley shifted. "Cory, come on—"

"No, Brad! Don't you remember what happened?"

"I do," Sam said. "You beat the shit out of me."

"Because you threw beer in my face."

"Because you talked shit about my dad."

"Your *dead* dad," Cory spat. He was right in Sam's face now, their noses just inches from each other. "He's dead. He can't hear me, so who am I hurting?"

Sam glanced past Cory and saw Bradley roll his eyes. Then he stared right at Cory and said, "Only yourself."

Cory's brows furrowed. "Wha—"

Before he could finish his meat-headed response, Sam brought his fist up and connected it with Cory's nose. Blood sprayed in droplets, most of it landing on Sam's face as Cory wheeled back and howled in pain. Bradley wrapped his arms around Cory, trying to keep him wrangled, but Cory was stronger and broke free from Bradley's grasp. He rushed Sam with the force of a linebacker, just like he had at the party.

But unlike the time at the party, Sam was ready for it. When Cory went for the tackle, Sam ducked out of the way, planted a hand on Cory's lower back, and used his momentum to shove the boy into the earth. Sam didn't wait to act further, getting down on the ground and straddling Cory's back, taking one of his arms and twisting it behind him.

"Ow, fuck!" Cory wailed.

Bradley came up behind them. "Jesus, Sam! Stop, you're gonna break his arm!" He tried to wrestle Cory's arm out of Sam's grasp, but Sam used his free hand to swipe blindly at Bradley, slapping him across the face a few times while tightening his grip on Cory. Sam heard Bradley retreat and he continued straining on Cory's arm.

He only stopped because someone stronger than him—it didn't take much—grabbed him and tossed him onto his back. Sam was now staring up at the sky, the warm light beating down and blinding him. The sun was eclipsed by a figure looming over him, casting a shadow across his vision. His eyes quickly adjusted to the lighting change and he saw that it was Ranger Denny. He didn't say anything, just looked down on Sam like everyone else in his life.

Ranger Denny grabbed Sam by the collar of his shirt and lifted him to his feet, then swiftly detained him by holding his hands at the wrists behind his back. Dazed by the sudden motion, Sam could only make out a blurry circle of faces surrounding him. The closest one of them was Bradley's, and when Sam's vision cleared up again, he could see that Bradley looked disappointed, not making eye contact with anything but the ground.

Everyone else, however, was either looking directly at Sam or down at Cory, who was still lying on his stomach. Mr. Veranda had arrived at the scene and went to Cory as Sam was being led away by the ranger, stumbling the whole time. Sam was glad that his old teacher hadn't seen what had gone down; he didn't think he could handle disappointing anyone else today.

🌲

Cory sat in the ranger's cabin, holding a piece of gauze to his dripping nose. The ranger told him to put as much pressure as he could on it so the bleeding would slow, but every time he touched his nose, he felt like he had to sneeze. And if he sneezed, wouldn't the bone come out, or pierce his brain or something? Either way, Cory knew it would be painful and resorted to holding the gauze just below his nose so the blood could drip onto it and not his new jeans. He didn't know why he cared about them anymore; Sam had already fucked them up by shoving him into the ground. *What an asshole,* Cory thought.

Ranger Vanessa walked out from the supply closet with a fresh strip of gauze. As she bent down and handed it to him, Cory peeked down her shirt and smirked when he saw a flash of her bra. "You can just toss that bloody one in the trash," she said. "Are you feeling okay?"

"Yeah, I suppose," Cory replied. "Better than before."

"Okay, emergency services should be here in ten minutes. Sit tight and let me know if you start to feel woozy."

Cory gave Ranger Vanessa a thumbs-up and she turned to go down the back hallway of the cabin. Cory watched her leave, his eyes tracking her ass as it swayed from side to side. He felt a pang of sadness when it disappeared around the corner, probably never to be seen again. Cory thought about calling her back solely for that reason. He'd be sure to tell the other guys about it whenever he got back from the hospital—but would they even care? They probably wouldn't talk to him ever again, now that he'd gotten his ass handed to him. Cory shook his head in disgust, but even that hurt to do.

Then he caught something out of the corner of his eye. He was sitting next to a window that faced the parking lot where a junker truck pulled in alongside their school bus. Cory watched as a man climbed out of the truck, went to the back seat to get something out of it, then close and lock the vehicle while walking toward the cabin. The man carried a bouquet of flowers in his hand, wrapped in bright blue plastic. As he got closer, Cory could see a morose expression on his face. Was he crying? What a pussy.

The man walked down the trail and followed the signs that pointed to the Ring, where the tour group had just gone. Now, Cory was planning to call ranger Vanessa back because he wasn't sure if he was hallucinating, or if what he'd just seen was real.

9

Two Months After

The worst part about it was they didn't even let him graduate. Sam was expelled two weeks before his last day of high school because of what happened on the field trip. He expected that, but he didn't expect to be so torn up about it. It felt like he was hit by a train when the school superintendent spoke the words to him, handed him the letter to bring to his parents—yes, she used the plural, she was that ignorant—and sent him on his way. When he took the letter in his shaky hand, he thought of Ms. Baker and Mr. Veranda, how disappointed they probably were in him. Sam almost wished he had taken his counselor's advice to apply himself, almost wished he would have taken another biology class.

And then there was his mother. There was no way he'd be allowed out of the house anymore, unless he did some serious negotiating. He would have to get a job, something he wasn't entirely against but avoided nonetheless. There was just nothing that interested him. Maybe Sam would get a job as a ranger at the park, pick up the trade like Denny and Vanessa had. Maybe he would finally develop that love for nature like his father had always hoped.

My dead father, Sam thought. He would never tell anyone, but he cried on his drive home on that last day of school.

His mother was livid. She lectured him for nearly a half hour, wondering how he could be so stupid, where she went wrong as a parent. The next ten minutes were reserved for an onslaught of questions about his plans from now on: "Are you going to finish school?" "Where are you going to work?" "Do you think I'm stupid?" "Did you know that *you're* stupid?" The whole ordeal was actually a lot milder than Sam had expected.

Of course, he already had the answer to every question his mother asked, but he didn't dare say them. *No. Probably some grocery store or something. A little, yes. A lot, yes.*

When she finally released him, she was sure to remind him that she loved him. Sam nodded and left the room, not reciprocating the feeling in any way. He just went to his room and started searching for jobs online. The one useful thing he got out of school was how to find work. He applied to multiple businesses, several of them grocery stores just to stick to his unspoken answers. Sam decided that he would accept whichever job got back to him first; it didn't matter much to him which one it happened to be since the pay was about the same across the board. Two days later he received an email from the mini-mart job he applied for, saying that it was his if he wanted it. He didn't, but he took it anyway.

On the first day of June, Sam was stocking shelves in the mini-mart with his coworker, Grayson. No one had come into the store for twenty minutes and the boys were growing tired of their solitude. Sam didn't know Grayson well enough to strike up a conversation with him. Grayson had worked at the mini-mart for two months before Sam started there, but in the week and a half they'd shared so far, they hardly mumbled a greeting to each other.

Now they were stuck together, sitting behind the checkout counter, silently waiting for someone to come in. Sam took to scrolling on his phone, the one his mother didn't know about and therefore couldn't confiscate. Grayson just stared at the floor. He couldn't be sure, but Sam didn't think Grayson had blinked once the entire time.

Finally, the bells that hung from the top of the door rang and shook Grayson and Sam from their unproductive state. Their attention was reserved for this person and this person only, having done everything else they needed to do.

This person, however, paid no attention to them, which was disheartening for the boys. The least he could've done was offer up a nod, but he did nothing of the sort. The man just breezed by the counter and made for the back of the store.

"That was rude," Grayson whispered.

"Totally," Sam replied. He thought about talking to Grayson some more, maybe asking him how he liked working here, but Grayson was already staring back at the floor.

The man returned to the counter a few minutes later with a case of beer and two bottles of vodka. Sam stood up and looked over the items. "Did you find everything you were looking for?" he asked.

The man nodded and reached into his back pocket for his wallet. He flipped it open and produced a credit card.

"Sorry, I need to look at your ID before you pay."

The man was confused. "Really?"

"It's store policy." Sam knew that the man was well over twenty-one and normally wouldn't care about double checking. But now that he was being paid to do it, the rules were the rules.

"I thought you would at least remember my face, Sam," the man said as he flicked his driver's license onto the counter. Sam picked it up and examined it, his eyes immediately going to the date of birth and determining the man was thirty-nine. Before he gave the card back, Sam looked at the man's name and was met with a wave of mixed feelings. His stomach dropped, but his mind wandered with family memories, the happy ones that Sam thought he'd lost long ago. How had he not recognized him?

"Hey, Darren," Sam said.

"There it is," his uncle replied, smiling. "How have you been?"

Sam shrugged. "Not too bad. Finally got a job, obviously."

"Good for you. It's important to start working young."

Sam scanned the alcohol's barcodes and Darren paid for it with a credit card. As he pulled it from the reader, Sam realized it was the same kind of credit card his mother used—he would know, because he took it all the time. "What's all this for, anyway? You having a party?"

Darren laughed a little. "Kind of. You know, you should swing by for it."

"Really?"

"Yeah, why not? I haven't seen you since your dad's service, and I don't remember the last time I got to hang out with my favorite nephew." When Sam gave Darren the receipt, he pulled a pen from his pocket and quickly scrawled his address on it. "Eight o'clock. Bring your friends." Darren took the beer and vodka and left the store, the bells jingling once again.

Sam had no idea how to feel about the invitation. On one hand, he hadn't seen Darren in over a year, and he was family after all. On the other, Sam's mother hated Darren and would freak out if she found out he'd gone to his house, much less talked to him in any capacity. He couldn't exactly avoid him at work; who would he be to turn a customer away? But this invite would be easier to decline. Maybe he had to work late, or he was grounded, or he really just didn't want to go. Darren wouldn't have to know the reason, and with all the alcohol he came in and bought, he might not even notice if Sam wasn't there.

But then he thought of his dad and how much he would want him to spend time with Darren. They would get together all the time when Sam was younger, play in the backyard, go out to dinner. He thought back on those memories fondly. Why did that ever change?

Having made up his mind about the party, Sam leaned against the counter. Darren had told him to bring friends, but he didn't have any of those. He looked to his left at the young man staring at the floor with his mouth hanging open and figured he would do just fine.

At eight o'clock exactly, Sam knocked on Darren's door. He stepped back, almost bumping into Grayson when he did, and looked up at the house. It was large, but in a modest sort of way, two stories with what looked to be a basement. Sam spotted a shed behind the house and wondered if that was how Darren made his living, fixing up cars or making cabinets out in the shop. The whole property was surrounded by trees, hiding the long driveway from the main road; Sam almost drove past it when he arrived. Now he stood on the doorstep with a bag of chips under his arm.

The door swung open and revealed a man Sam had never seen before. His red hair hung just over his eyes, and he brushed away to see who was at the door. "Oh, you must be Darren's nephew," the man said. He leaned back into the house and yelled to tell

Darren his guests were there. Then he stuck out his hand and faced Sam. "I'm Cherry."

Sam shook Cherry's hand. "Sam."

"I know. Darren wouldn't shut up about seeing you today." Cherry stepped to the side and gestured for the boys to come in. Sam did, but it took Grayson a few seconds to follow.

Sam smelled smoke the second he stepped into the house. It wasn't the normal cigarette kind he smelled whenever his mother smoked, but one that was more putrid, like skunk. Sam scrunched up his nose and elected to breathe through his mouth as much as he could. Grayson, on the other hand, inhaled deeply and sighed as if he was smelling a fragrant rose. "Love that smell," he said.

"Just you wait, my friend," said Cherry. He led them to the basement stairwell, which looked a little hazy and stunk worse than the entryway of the house. Sam looked over his shoulder at Grayson, who had the most enthusiasm Sam had ever seen, like a kid on Christmas Day. Cherry descended the stairs and the boys followed him, the wood creaking beneath their feet. The further down they went, the less finished the house around them became. Painted walls gave way to bare studs without insulation between them. The floor was smooth concrete, barely visible under all the trash strewn about the expanse of the basement. A miniature basketball hoop hung next to a dart board on the wall, a pool table the only furniture in sight. That was until Sam looked to the other side of the basement where he saw Darren sitting on a couch.

"Sam! So glad you decided to come!" Darren stood up from the leather couch, having a bit of a hard time getting out of its cushy grasp. Once he did, he stumbled over to his nephew and patted him on the shoulder. "And this is your coworker, right?" Darren asked, looking past Sam.

"I'm Grayson. This place is awesome!"

"You ain't seen nothing yet! Come, sit down!" Darren went back to his spot on the couch. Cherry sat next to him and another man Sam hadn't noticed until he sat down was in a chair in the corner. The entire sitting area was set around a coffee table with an ornate rug underneath it. "I take it you already met Cherry. That over there is Vic." He pointed to the man in the corner, who gave a tired wave. "Don't take any shit from him. Bitch works at a diner." Darren laughed until he saw Vic's evil eye he was sending his way. "Sorry, you've caught us at an... interesting time."

"We pregamed," said Vic, brushing off the insult. "Hope you don't mind."

Sam wasn't sure what Vic meant, but Grayson seemed to be right in his element. "Oh, it's all good," he said without missing a beat. "As long as I get to catch up to you guys!"

Vic smiled and nodded his head. "I like this kid." He reached over to the end table next to him and picked up a beer can, offering it silently to Sam. When he declined, Grayson took the beer off Vic's hands and put it into his own, nearly shaking with excitement as he opened the can and started chugging.

"Oh, man," Darren said, "you're gonna have to do a lot more than that if you want to get to our level."

Grayson stopped long enough to take a breath, then went right back to drinking the beer until it was empty. Sam was almost impressed with him, but then his coworker burped obnoxiously and ruined any awe he had. Darren, Cherry, and Vic, though, all started laughing and saying repeatedly how good of a burp it was. After a little while of enduring Cherry's laugh—some hilarious mixture of a chuckle and a guffaw—Sam joined in on the humor and began laughing himself. "I bet I can beat that," he said, motioning for Vic to pass him a beer.

"Oh, we have a challenger!" Darren said. "Show him who's boss, Sam!"

Sam cracked the can open and hesitated for a moment. He never had beer before, at least not in recent memory. There was probably a time when his mom or dad let him have a sip, but that point in history, marked by his father's presence, was long ago. He cast the nostalgia away and pounded the beer back, the odd taste washing across his tongue. He almost stopped, let himself breathe as Grayson did, but he kept drinking despite his body's signals to stop. Sam didn't like what was happening, the feeling he was getting, the way everyone was yelling at him to keep chugging. But he kept going anyway and didn't stop until the last few drops entered his mouth.

Then he let out the most rancid burp he'd ever heard, which was followed up by a cacophony of laughter from the audience of his coworker, his uncle, and his uncle's cronies. Sam was never one to laugh at a bodily sound; he held himself to a higher standard than that. Sure, he would've thought a fart was funny in elementary school, but now that he was a working adult, he didn't find the humor in gas. Even so, Sam found himself laughing along with the men around him, not even questioning his maturity.

"He's a natural!" Vic said. "Darren, I think it's time to light up."

Darren's face hardened and he shook his head. "I don't know. They're just kids, I don't want to fuck up their brains."

"Come on, man," said Grayson, "I've smoked before."

"What have you smoked?"

"What do you mean? Weed, of course."

Darren laughed, which made Sam nervous. He watched as his uncle pulled a piece of molded glass from his pocket. "We're not talking about weed, son."

"Oh, shit." Grayson's face went blank. "You guys are... wow."

"Yeah." Darren raised the piece of glass to his face and pulled out a lighter, flicking the flame into existence and placing it just below the bulb at the other end of the glass. His hand shook and Sam could hear something inside the bulb rattle against it, but as Darren held the flame to the glass, the rattling ceased. When it did, he put the glass into his mouth and inhaled, holding his breath for a moment and then exhaling a cloud of smoke. That's when Sam realized what the piece of glass was, and had a pretty good hunch about what was inside it.

"Alright, hand it over," Grayson said.

Darren didn't budge, just stared at Grayson and sucked in his cheeks. "I don't know, kid. This is a new piece. I made Cherry buy me a new one because my old one broke when I threw it at his head."

"Just gimme it. It'll make a hell of a story."

Darren cocked his head, smiled a little bit, and nodded. "Fine," Darren said, "but you didn't get it from me."

Both of them leaned toward each other and the exchange was made, Grayson flopping back onto the couch next to Sam with the pipe and the lighter. He did the same thing that Darren did, trying to take a longer hit to show him up, but ended up in a coughing fit. Darren, Vic, and Cherry started laughing again while Grayson tried to stop coughing. Sam noticed they were deep and dry, and at the end of it all, Grayson's eyes were watering, face red, lips chapped and stuck in a stupid position. He looked like he was going to puke.

But then he let out a little laugh. "Guess I flew too close to the sun."

"Nice one, Icarus," Sam said.

Grayson looked at him, confused. "Huh?"

"Nothing," replied Sam. "Okay, my turn."

"Whoa, hey," Darren said with his arms outstretched to Sam. "I don't know if that's a good idea."

"Why? Grayson did it."

"Yeah, but Grayson's mom doesn't hate me. If I send you back to her higher than a kite, what's she gonna think of me? She'll never let you out of the house again, and I'll probably get jailed."

Sam shook his head. "She'll never know. I've lied to her about tons of things, and by now she's too tired to press me on them."

"Sam..."

Darren's look was dire. Sam felt like he was staring into his soul, into his past at something far beyond himself. It was invasive, but not in a bad way. It was actually comforting for Sam, which only made him want to do it more. He took the pipe and lighter from Grayson. "I'll be fine, I promise."

It wasn't at all what he thought it would be like. When he inhaled, it was just like any other breath, just a little bit warmer and a different flavor. Sam never thought he'd be concerned about the air's flavor, but here he was, feeling like he was sucking up smoke from a fireplace. Was there a fireplace in here? He looked around and saw there wasn't and kept wondering why he was sweating. His vision seemed to sharpen, but only on the thing he was looking at directly; everything else was blurry.

"How do you feel?"

Sam blinked hard and tried to figure out who was talking to him. He looked around the room wildly, but recognized none of the faces that were pointed at him. Still, he thought he should address the disembodied voice. "I feel fine," he said. "I feel—"

All at once he started coughing, just like Grayson had. He understood why Grayson had looked like he was in pain the whole time—Sam was experiencing that same anguish. His lungs were erupting with fire in short, powerful spurts. His diaphragm was worked to the point of aching, his head pounding from the pressure within his body. Sam managed to stop for a moment, draw in a deep breath before coughing again. Only this time, it wasn't just air that came out.

Sam threw up on the concrete floor. It was mostly liquid and very foamy from all the beer. Grayson quickly shifted his feet so they didn't get in the way of the stream. The bile splashed onto the rug under the coffee table and soaked into it while Sam sat, hunched over and feeling defeated.

"Fuck, little dude!" Vic yelled.

"The fucking carpet!" screamed Cherry.

Darren rounded the table and ran up the stairs. He came back a few minutes later with some towels and a bucket of soapy water. He got down on his hands and knees and started soaking up Sam's puke.

"Ah, no Darren," Sam said, "I can do it." He knelt on the floor and grabbed one of the smaller towels. After dunking it into the bucket, he rubbed the towel across the carpet. It began to froth up and Sam became increasingly aware of how the wet towel felt on his wrinkly hands. He started scrubbing harder; he had to get the puke out of the rug. How could he have done this? Why did it have to be on the rug? It could be soaked up easily on the concrete, but the *rug*? What was he thinking? He had to get the puke out, he had to, it had to get clean…

"Scrub, scrub, scrub…"

Sam heard someone chanting behind him. He turned around and recognized Grayson, sitting on the couch and hitting his closed hands against his thighs while cheering Sam on. Soon enough, Vic started going along with it in the corner, cracking open another beer and chanting with Grayson in between sips. Sam smirked and started scrubbing the rug harder and faster. It was getting warm from the friction.

"Scrub, scrub, scrub!"

The chanting was louder now that Cherry had joined in. Even Darren, who just finished wiping up the vomit from the floor, was starting to give Sam encouragement.

"Scrub! Scrub! Scrub!"

Sam had no idea why the chanting was making him feel better. All he knew was that he was a cleaning machine, going hard at the spot on the rug, constantly rinsing the towel in the bucket of warm water. The soap was made to smell like apples, but because it was mixing with the acidic scent of Sam's puke, the air was filled with a revolting—but simultaneously enticing—aroma. Sam couldn't figure out if he liked it or not, but it didn't matter to him. Not now. Not when he was being chanted to.

They care about me. I can't believe it.

"Scrub! Scrub! Scrub!"

10

One Month Before

That wasn't the last time Sam went to Darren's house. His uncle held multiple other parties after the first one Sam attended. There were more people at a few of them, friends of Darren's but strangers to Sam. He wasn't sure why, but he always brought Grayson along with him. Sam thought it was because it made himself look better when Grayson was sat next to him, mouth hanging open and belching up a storm. But even though he wasn't the brightest or the best friend of Sam's, Grayson still brought a little bit of comfort with him. He wasn't a stranger, and that's what made Sam stick by his side throughout all the get togethers Darren threw. That, and the fact that Sam felt better about himself and his life choices when Grayson was across the room, attempting a keg stand or taking a blinker off of someone's pen.

It wasn't that Sam was against drugs and alcohol; in fact, the more he hung around with Darren, the more accustomed to them he became. He understood why people would go out on the weekends and have too much to drink, crowd into someone's basement and sit in a circle to pass a joint around. Sam couldn't see himself doing it every weekend, but the appeal was obvious. He ended up going to six of Darren's parties before his mother started questioning where her son was going at night.

"I'm just hanging out with Grayson," Sam said, which wasn't a total lie.

His mom scowled. "Who is that?"

"My coworker at the mini-mart. I go to his house sometimes after work."

"Do his parents know?"

"He's twenty."

"Oh." She thought for a moment, leaning against the kitchen table. "He doesn't drink, does he?"

"Mom..."

"Well, what should I expect from someone I've never met? That he's a totally upstanding citizen? Come on, Sam, he works at the mini-mart!"

"*I* work at the mini-mart, mom."

"Well, you're different."

Sam was starting to regret spinning this lie in the first place. "He's fine, mom. You have nothing to worry about."

That statement *was* a total lie.

Sam knew this, of course; he would never cause his mother distress on purpose, which is why he thought it was better not to tell her about Darren. His tactics worked for a while, long enough for Sam to go to two more of his uncle's parties without his mother knowing. But on Memorial Day weekend, an envelope showed up in the mix of mail that neither Sam nor his mother was expecting.

"Oh, what does he want now?" Sam's mom asked. "He knows he can just text us. I don't even want to open this. I should just burn it."

"I'll open it," Sam said. "I don't think either of us should be near a flame right now." He laughed on the inside, because he used a lighter to smoke just the other day. He ripped open the envelope and took out the folded piece of paper inside. It was printer paper covered in clip art of eagles and fireworks. Uncle Sam and the American flag made up most of the background, the words on top of the image almost unreadable. Sam did his best to recite them to his mom. "'You're invited to Darren's Fourth of July Bash. Party will start at noon and will keep going until the freedom bell stops ringing.'" He looked at his mom. "What is this?"

"We get the same invite every year," Sam's mother explained, "and your father always insisted that we go. I drove you in the van so we could leave whenever we wanted."

"I don't remember a party last year."

His mother gave him a blank expression, and then it clicked in Sam's mind that he didn't remember a party because there wasn't one, because his father had died. "Oh. Right. Well, are we going this year?"

"I don't want to. Even after all this time, I don't think I could stand seeing him." She looked at him, shook her head. "But you're an adult now, Sam. I'm not going to keep you from doing what you want."

"Who said I wanted to go?"

"I can see it on your face. I don't know why, but you want to go, and I'm not going to stop you."

Sam couldn't deny that he wanted to go to the party. After going to so many over the weeks, he actually grew closer to his uncle Darren. He reminded him of his father in the way he talked, walked and carried himself, even the way he drank from a beer bottle was the same. Sam felt like he was getting closer to his father through his uncle, who was arguably the closest thing to a father he had left.

"Okay," he finally said after thinking silently for a while. "I'll bring back a hot dog for you or something."

His mother laughed. "Yeah, okay."

Grayson picked Sam up to go to Darren's party at quarter to eleven. Weeks ago, when the two young men had first met each other, the drive would have been awkward. Neither of them would have said a word other than "hi," the radio would probably be off because neither knew what music the other liked. Now, though, they scream-sang to the awful country songs that Grayson liked and that Sam tolerated because Grayson liked them. He never tried when he sang, the pitch of his voice so far off from that of the music. Sam didn't care, though. This was his way of entertaining himself: singing badly to songs he hated.

The first time he'd done this was with his father—they were making fun of a terrible pop song Sam's mother had stuck in her head one day—and now, whenever he does it, he thinks of him. As he and Grayson pulled into Darren's driveway, Sam wondered if his father and uncle had ever sang badly to an annoying song. He could imagine them doing it, his dad driving and Darren in the passenger seat, both of them dangerously young. One of them would reach over and crank the volume dial and the music would go from obnoxious to deafening, so loud that their terrible singing would be drowned out by the very song they were trying to imitate. But they would try to overpower it anyway, until their voices were raw and ears were ringing.

Grayson parked the car behind one of many others that lined Darren's long, secluded driveway. Sam was surprised that someone like Darren would live this far from the city, where all the party people normally chose to reside. He supposed there were other factors that kept him way out here away from everything. Work was probably one of them, although Sam had no idea what his uncle did to afford this property.

They got out of the car and could hear faint music playing in the backyard. Sam wasn't sure, but he thought it might be the same song he and Grayson were scream-singing to just minutes ago. They made their way to the other side of the house and quickly realized this was the largest party Darren had thrown yet. Sam looked across the expansive back lawn and saw at least forty people scattered across it. Some of them were playing yard games, others sat around a small fire pit—but no matter what everyone was doing, they did it with a drink in their hand.

"Bitchin'," Grayson uttered softly.

Sam's head spun to his right when he heard the sound of a sliding patio door. In the doorway stood Darren, wearing sunglasses and a red, white, and blue vest with no undershirt. His khaki shorts swished as he walked to the edge of the wooden porch and waved enthusiastically at Sam and Grayson. "Hey there, boys! How's this for a party?"

"It looks great," Sam said, actually meaning it. He didn't think he'd ever find joy in a party like this, especially after the fiasco that went down last summer. He was sure today would be a fun one as long as he didn't need to fight anybody. "Are we late?"

"No, no, you're right on time. Go get yourselves something to drink, mix and mingle a little bit. Vic and Cherry are playing horseshoe toss if you want to join them. I'll come find you guys in a second." Darren walked over to a group of people sitting in lawn chairs and leaned on the back of one of them, starting a conversation Sam couldn't hear.

Grayson immediately made for the coolers, popping each one of them open until he found something he liked. Sam followed suit, but instead of sifting through icy water for alcohol, he went for the cooler with soda and bottled water in it. He pulled out a sweaty bottle, unscrewed the cap, and took a few sips before noticing Grayson's disgust. "Come on, dude. Water?"

"I'm starting slow," Sam said. "Plus, shouldn't one of us stay just a little bit sober so we can get home?"

Grayson nodded and held out his beer. Sam touched his water bottle to it and they both drank. "To America's birthday," Grayson said. He started laughing a little bit. "Hey, do you think other countries do Fourth of July?"

"Probably not."

"Huh. I don't see why not. This is fuckin' sweet!" He took another swig of beer, then started scanning the faces of the party. "Let's go find Vic and Cherry. I wanna smoke 'em in horseshoes."

They made their way to the pits where the two men stood, throwing horseshoes and getting increasingly angry with themselves. "Why the fuck do people even play this game?" said Vic before he noticed Sam and Grayson.

"I'll show you how it's done," Grayson said, stepping up behind Vic and taking the horseshoe out of his hand.

"Oh, sure. Big horseshoes guy over here!"

Sam watched as Grayson wound up for the underhand throw, then sent the piece of metal flying through the air, rotating gracefully until it wrapped itself around the length of rebar stuck in the dirt. It clanged down and thumped into the dirt, sending up a cloud of dust before coming to a complete stop.

"Yeah," Grayson retorted, "big horseshoes guy."

"Yo, how'd you do that?" Cherry called from the other pit. "I want that kid on my team."

"You're on," said Vic. He turned to Sam. "You know how to throw, Scrub?"

That nickname, Sam thought. He didn't care how funny the story was to them, it was embarrassing for him. He sighed and said, "I'll do my best. How is it scored?"

Vic explained the rules as he walked over to Cherry. "Three points for every shoe around the stake, two for every shoe that touches the stake or is within a thumb's length. Normally it's one point for that, but we fuckin' suck."

"Got it." Sam picked up the two horseshoes out of the dirt and held them in front of Grayson. "Do you want to throw first?"

"Nah man, that's all you."

Sam took his stance beside the post and eyed the one twenty feet away. He exhaled as he tried to replicate what he saw Grayson do with his warm-up, swinging his arm behind him, gripping the horseshoe lightly with his fingertips. He let go at the apex of his swing and the horseshoe flipped end-over-end, then stuck in the earth by the prongs and stayed there. It wasn't even close to the stake, and he heard Grayson stifle a laugh. Sam threw him an accusatory glance and Grayson stiffened up. "Don't worry, you got another chance."

Sam set himself back up, knowing that he needed to put more strength behind this throw. He wound up again and then tossed the horseshoe. This one landed much closer to the stake than the last, so much so that Vic had to bend down and stick out his thumb for measurement. "That's three points for us!" he yelled.

"Three?" Cherry asked. "What are you talking about?"

"Two points for this one, and one for that one." Vic pointed to the horseshoe stuck in the ground. "That's gotta be worth something."

"It's not, you shit."

"You're a shit!"

"Am not!"

"Are too!"

Cherry and Vic started shoving each other, both throwing palms at shoulders hoping to topple their opponent, which was an easy task considering neither of them were sober. It wasn't long before both of them were on the ground, wrestling and trying to get on top of one another but failing miserably. Sam and Grayson looked on at them, pointing and laughing, waving at other people to come and see what was going on. A small crowd gathered just as Cherry pinned Vic to the ground, then collapsed on top of him from exhaustion.

"What the hell is this?" Darren asked, weaving through the people to get to Sam. "Oh, they finally fucked, huh? We all knew it, right guys?" The crowd whooped and cheered in agreement and Sam shifted a little bit. He wasn't sure why, but Darren's comment made him deeply uncomfortable. The feeling left as quickly as it came when Darren clapped his hand on Sam's back. "Did you win?"

"I scored two points," said Sam, "but Vic thought I got three."

Darren's gaze traveled to the other horseshoe pit, first landing on the heap of men laying in the grass, and then to Sam's first attempt sticking up out of it. "Holy shit! Did you do that? That's gotta be worth five points, at least!"

"It's not worth shit!" Cherry yelled, his words somewhat muffled from being spoken into Vic's chest.

"Would you get the fuck up already?" Darren leaned in and whispered to Sam and Grayson. "I got something to talk to you boys about."

"What's up?"

Darren took a quick glance around and shook his head. "It's best I tell you in private. All I'll say now is that it's a business opportunity, and I have a feeling you guys'll wanna get in on it."

"Shit, I'm in," Grayson said a little too loudly for Darren's liking. He was promptly shushed and mouthed an apology soon after.

"Let's go to the shed," Darren suggested. "We can pick those two up on the way."

He started for the shed, which was hidden behind a wall of trees. Sam and Grayson followed blindly and Darren lifted Cherry off the ground by the collar, the limp drunk not really helping the effort. Vic was more willful in getting up and got to his feet all by himself, then proceeded to stumble all the way to the shed.

Sam, the only sober one out of the five of them, walked a little slower than everyone else. His mind raced with the possibilities of what his uncle had meant by "business opportunity." Did he want to start a drug ring? Sam didn't know if he was ready for that; he barely even did any drugs to begin with. How could he sell them to people? He'd seen the movies and TV shows about the cartel, and every one that came to mind involved multiple—if not all—of the main characters getting shot or dying. Sam wasn't sure if it was just him being a pussy, but he wanted no part in being on either side of a gun.

He shook the nervous thoughts away when he broke through the wall of trees. It couldn't possibly be as bad as he was imagining it. Darren was family, and Sam liked to think that he would never put his nephew in danger like that. And after today, Sam could finally stop wondering what Darren did for work.

11

Three and a Half Weeks Before

It was Chief Nell who gave Denny the confidence he needed to finally ask Vanessa on a formal date. "Son," Nell had said, "you can't just dangle a line in the water and hope for a bite."

"Isn't that literally all fishing is?" Denny asked.

The chief ranger shook his head. "In order to actually catch anything, Oh Uh Denny, you need to throw some bait on the hook."

Denny sighed. "I find it concerning that I'm starting to understand your metaphors."

"You'll have to deal with it. They're about as close to going away as I am to stop giving a shit about this park. Let's go check on those burls."

They did and found nothing out of the ordinary, which had been the norm since April. That was the maddest Denny had ever seen Chief Nell; a heist right under their noses after such a long notheft streak. They were lucky there weren't any families in the area, or else the children would have learned some brand-new words.

After their burl check, Denny went to find Vanessa—the chief made sure to cover for him to "be a good wingman." He found her in the ranger cabin's break room and sat down across from her. "Hi," Denny started off with.

"Hi," Vanessa repeated.

"How's your day going so far?"

"Not too bad. I did have to chase a couple out of the park, though. I don't know what it is about this time of the year that makes people think it's suddenly okay to have sex in the woods. I mean, you can do it, just not here."

"You actually can't do it anywhere," Denny said. "That's public indecency."

"It's disgusting is what it is. Just think about it: you're out in nature, surrounded by a bunch of plants and shit that could give you rashes in the worst possible places. And what if a bear ran up on you? You'd get mauled before you could even pull your pants up."

Denny was laughing too hard to offer a response. He actually had to wipe a tear from his eye before he could start talking again. "Ahh, yeah. People are stupid." He questioned if his reaction was genuine or played-up in order to get her to like him.

"Tell me about it," Vanessa said as she leaned back in her chair. Its creaking was the only sound in the room. She pursed her lips, drummed on her thighs a bit before setting the chair back on all four legs. She and Denny exchanged awkward glances until the sound of an alarm cut through the silence. Vanessa pulled her phone from her pocket and shook her head. "Break's over. Gotta get back out there."

"Right," said Denny. He watched Vanessa stand up from the table and walk away, all the while psyching himself up to do what he came in here to do. She was just out of the doorway when he spoke up. "Hey, Vanessa?"

She poked her head back into the break room. "What's up?"

Denny shook. He knew what he wanted to say and had a clear chance to do it—so why was it so hard to get the words out? He knew that there was something going on between them, something that had the potential of growing into something else. Denny wanted that to happen, even if it was the slimmest chance. So he inhaled, doing his best to hide his nerves and hope the sweat in his armpits wasn't noticeable. "Would you like to go out sometime?"

Vanessa cocked her head and leaned back into the doorway. "Like on a date?"

"Sure," Denny said without really thinking. He watched her face, saw it tick with thought. Her eyes rolled ever so slightly, lips quivering while trying to form words. Maybe she was more nervous than Denny was.

"Yeah," Vanessa said, her lips now curling into a smile. "I think that would be nice."

Denny matched her expression and nodded his head. "Cool. When, uh—"

But Vanessa had already turned away and started walking down the hallway. "We'll talk after work!"

"Okay!" He finally let himself breathe; he hadn't even noticed he was holding air in. It made sense, though, with how nervous he was. Why was he nervous, exactly? He knew Vanessa liked him, or else she wouldn't have agreed to go on a date. But what if she was just doing it to appease him? What if this would be their first and only date, then after Denny had already paid for dinner or the movie or whatever the hell they'd done, Vanessa would pat him on the shoulder and give him the classic "It's not you, it's me." Every day of work would be awkward from then on! What would they say in passing? Would they even acknowledge each other? Had Denny made a huge mistake in asking Vanessa out?

Now, instead of holding his breath, he was hyperventilating. He shut his eyes hard, then blinked a few times and slowed his breathing until he calmed down. When he looked up at the doorway, Denny saw Chief Nell standing in it. He looked concerned.

"What?" Denny asked.

"Are you kidding me? You look like you're about to cry. Did she say no?"

Denny swallowed, only now realizing how dry his mouth was. "She said yes."

"Ah, now your tizzy makes sense," Nell said sarcastically. "What's the big deal? I've overheard you two talking, and let me tell you, there's some sparks—"

"Hold on, you've been spying on us?"

"No, you guys just talk loud as hell. I may be old, but I have ears like a dog. And those ears hear you and Vanessa flirting with each other every time you get the chance. You like her, Denny, and she likes you." Chief Nell snorted. "God, you're the first guy I've ever seen so worked up over a girl taking interest in him. What's wrong with you, kid?"

Denny laughed. "Shut up, *Henry*." He knew using the chief's full name might land him in hot water, but it was worth it to see the shock on his face. "Go count your burls."

"How about Chinese?"

Denny bobbed his head from side to side. "I'm not really a fan. It's a very specific taste that I don't like a whole lot."

Vanessa scoffed. "You're nuts! What about orange chicken? You *have* to like orange chicken."

"I don't *have* to like anything. I will say that Panda Palace's orange chicken is to die for."

"Okay, but that's not authentic."

Denny shrugged. "Still tastes good."

Vanessa shifted in the passenger's seat. "I'll get through to you one day."

Any other day, Denny would be driving in silence. He never liked having the radio on while he was on the road, and whenever he tried, he'd always get distracted with skipping through different stations, trying to find the right song. Now, though, he was distracted for an entirely different reason: the beautiful girl sitting next to him. Vanessa knew about his odd driving habits, as they'd carpooled to the park a few times in the past. Normally she would respect Denny's wishes and not touch the radio dial, but tonight she hooked up her phone to the speaker system and shuffled one of her playlists. She kept the volume low and, surprisingly, Denny didn't mind the background noise. In fact, he found it quite delightful.

"Ooh!" Vanessa said. "Pasta! How have we not thought about pasta?"

"I'd be okay with that."

"Great. I know a place around here, you'll love it." She directed Denny through a series of turns—some of which Denny missed—until he pulled into the parking lot of a small diner. The lights inside the building shone out against the evening sky, the nearly full-glass wall revealing a quaint setting with a few people sitting and eating. They got out of the car and walked up to the diner's door, Denny holding it open for Vanessa like a true gentleman.

When they entered, the waiter behind the counter quickly sprang up from his slumped position, no doubt bored by the slow night he'd been having. "Welcome," he said, feigning excitement. "Can I get you guys some menus? Something to drink?"

"I'll just have water," Denny said, sitting down at the counter.

"Make that two," said Vanessa. She took a menu and gave it to Denny. "How is it tonight, Victor?"

The waiter perked up a bit and did a double-take at the woman sitting in front of him. "Oh, hey Vanessa. Can't complain." Victor grabbed two cups and scooped ice into each of them, then picked up the tap and filled them with water before sliding the cups in front of his patrons. "There you go, let me know when you're ready to order." He walked out from behind the counter and crossed to a table on the far side of the diner, delivering a check to a party of three.

Denny watched Victor leave, then looked back at the menu. "Come here often enough to know the waiter's name?" he asked Vanessa while he scanned the food options.

"Sort of. He's an old friend. I come visit him here once in a while." She took a sip of water, her eyes never meeting Denny's.

"From high school?"

Vanessa sighed and set her cup down. "He's an ex," she said in a hushed tone. "Don't worry, it was a while ago, and it ended on good terms for the most part."

Denny tensed up. "For the most part? I'm sorry to press, but…"

"No, it's fine. It was a little messy for a while, but he got over it." She took the menu out of Denny's hands and looked it over. "Why are we even looking at this this?" Vanessa snapped her fingers and called over to Victor. "Oh, waiter! We would like some of your finest chicken Alfredo."

Denny was so flustered that he couldn't even tell her that he'd lost his appetite. Vanessa had ordered them a big plate of pasta to share, but when it came, Denny had about two forkfuls before his stomach started protesting. Victor only bothered them to give them their check, which Denny paid for, of course. But sometimes, Denny could see the waiter glancing over at them, his eyes moving from him to Vanessa to the dirty dishes at the booth a few tables down. Victor's shiftiness made him feel uneasy, like he was plotting something. Denny wished he could figure out what it was.

When he and Vanessa stood up to leave, Victor called to them just before they got out the door. "Hey, are you still working at that park?"

"Yeah," Vanessa said, "we both are." She slipped her hand in the crook of Denny's elbow, pulling him close to her.

Victor nodded. "Cool. Maybe I'll come in for a tour someday."

"That would be great. We'd love to show you around." Vanessa turned, preparing to leave the diner, but Denny stayed in place for a few moments more.

"Nice meeting you, Victor," he said.

Victor just nodded and waved goodbye.

Sam pulled the mini-mart door open, the bells hung on it jingling upon his entrance. Grayson was already behind the counter, which Sam thought was unusual. He almost always got to work before Grayson, even on the days that they carpooled—Grayson would stay in the car and text people until he absolutely had to come in.

What wasn't unusual, however, was how tired Grayson looked. Sam almost didn't see him there with his head laying down on the counter.

"Long night?" Sam asked him.

"I got three hours of sleep," he replied, not even lifting his head.

"Dude, what do you do all night?"

"Watch videos and stuff. Play games."

"With who?"

Grayson shrugged, but it just looked like his body jerked forward. "People."

"Whatever. Is Missy in yet?"

"Not sure, why?"

"We have to ask for time off."

Grayson didn't say anything, just turned his head so he was now resting his chin on the counter instead of his cheek. "Huh?"

"We have to ask off, remember? For Darren?"

It took him a little bit, but Grayson's brain eventually deciphered what Sam was saying. "Ohhh, right. Yeah, you get right on that, Scrub." Without another word, he closed his eyes and started breathing heavily, which turned into over-the-top fake snoring.

"Dork," said Sam. He left Grayson at the counter and went to the back of the store to Missy's office. The door was opened just a crack when Sam knocked on it and a raspy voice beckoned him to come in. "Hey, Missy."

She acknowledged him, her silver wisps of hair seemingly waving to him before she looked back down at the papers on her desk. "What's up, Sam?"

"Nothing much. I was just coming in to ask if Grayson and I are good to take a day off in a couple weeks."

Missy met Sam's eyes, looking over her bifocals that sat on the end of her nose. "What day?"

"Just the twenty-eighth. I think it's a Friday."

"You're gonna take a three day weekend?"

"I guess so. My mom and I are going on a little vacation, a sort of mother and son thing."

"Why is Grayson coming with you?"

"He's not. He just wants a day off and is too scared to ask for it himself." Sam knew the excuse was dumb at best, but it was all he had.

"Yeah, sounds like him," Missy said. She shifted the papers on her desk and pulled up what looked to be a calendar. "I'll mark you both down and get someone else to cover your shifts."

"Thank you so much, Missy."

"And tell Grayson to get off his ass and wake up already. Slap him if you have to."

Sam smiled as he left the room. "Will do."

12

FIFTEEN MINUTES BEFORE

Riding in the backseat of his uncle's truck with four other people on the way to cut some rare wood off one of the most protected trees in the country was something Sam never thought he would have on his to-do list. Nevertheless, he was there, sandwiched in between Grayson and Cherry with his legs scrunched up to his chest. Whenever Vic turned the steering wheel even the slightest bit, Sam would lean heavily to one side and bump shoulders with the men on either side of him. He tried to stop that from happening, but no amount of strength and straining could keep him in his middle seat for long. Sam learned to accept it after ten minutes on the road, but still wished that he at least had a seat belt across his chest to keep him in place.

Looking out the window on Grayson's side, Sam could see the tree line starting to get taller. He remembered that this is how it had been on the field trip, only then he had a seat all to himself. With his ear turned to the back of the truck, he could hear the equipment rattling around in the bed.

"Grayson, did you tie the stuff down like I told you to?" Darren asked from the front seat. Apparently he had heard the rattling as well.

"Yeah," Grayson said. He turned to Sam and mouthed, "*No.*"

Sam noticed that Darren was getting increasingly frustrated with Grayson over the past few weeks. Even at the Fourth of July party, Darren was trying to explain a rough outline of the plan to everyone and kept having to repeat it for Grayson to catch up. After saying the same thing three times, Darren just said "fuck it" and put Grayson on a need-to-know basis. Sam wasn't sure it was the best idea; if Grayson really was the dimmest among them, shouldn't he be the most informed?

"I know what you mean, Scrub," Darren said when Sam brought this up to him. "But how is he gonna get informed if he doesn't listen to what I'm saying? His skull's too thick, it grew into his ears and plugged them up!"

Darren had said all of this with Grayson in rather close proximity, but he never reacted to any of it. That only proved Darren's point further.

When the trees started getting redder as well as taller, Darren turned in his seat to face the group as best as he could. "Alright, it's the big day," he said. "Hasn't rained in a while, so it should be pretty easy for us to lug out without all that water weight. Also means easy cutting, for the most part. That'll be up to Cherry, like always. I brought along a shovel so we can lift the thing up and get the rope around it so we can pull it out of the forest easy-peasy."

"As if it's not gonna weigh a hundred pounds," said Cherry.

"It won't be that much if we're all pulling. It'll be twenty-five for each of us. What, you don't think you can pull twenty-five pounds behind you, Cherry?"

"I'm not sure that's how it—"

"Yeah," Darren interrupted. "Didn't think so. I bet I could pull more than you, even with my fucked-up shoulder."

They drove in silence for a few more miles, the trees along the road still growing taller the further they went. Eventually the height of the forest plateaued and Vic started slowing down. As the truck began its halt, Sam became acutely aware of his breathing and how it seemed to be doing the opposite of what the truck was doing. He tried to hide it, calm himself down before Grayson or Cherry noticed that he was freaking out. It was quieter when he breathed through his mouth rather than his nose, but then Sam worried that his breath was bad and that he was pumping out disgusting air into the cab of the truck. He made himself yawn, which put a pause on his hyperventilation long enough to compose himself. He closed his eyes as the truck stopped and everyone prepared to get out. Sam climbed out of the truck last, rounding to the tailgate behind Grayson.

Darren tugged on the handle and the tailgate flipped down, the slow-release system not doing its job whatsoever as the gate slammed open. In the open truck bed lay the scattered tools, all bound loosely with the long rope. "Grayson," Darren said, "what the hell is this?"

"The knot must have come undone."

"Bullshit. If you would've done it like I showed you, it would be fine!"

"I thought I did it like that."

Darren just sighed and shook his head. "You're lucky we need your help pulling it out, or else I'd make you stay with Vic." He climbed up into the truck bed and retrieved the shovel and chainsaw, bringing them back to the tailgate with him. Cherry took the chainsaw and handed the shovel to Grayson.

"Do you need me to take anything?" Sam asked. Then, whispering, "Maybe I should carry the shovel?"

Cherry shook his head. "Let him have it. It'll make him feel needed."

Darren unwound the tangled rope and tossed it down to Sam. "It's not just for pulling the burl out," he explained. "We're all gonna hold onto it like a bunch of kindergartners, so we don't get lost. There's no trail from our entry point, and soon it'll be almost too dark to see." Darren made quick eye contact with Sam and Cherry, but lingered for a bit on Grayson. "Never let go of the rope, you hear? Not until we reach the tree."

"Which tree are we hitting?" Grayson asked.

"You're on thin fucking ice, kid. Didn't I tell you not to ask questions? You'll know when we get there, maybe." Darren took one end of the rope and, as he filed in behind him, Sam heard his uncle mumble, "Unless you're too stupid to know that, too."

Sam felt his phone buzz in his pocket, which was odd to him because he never had it silenced before today. It made sense, though; there would already be so much noise with the chainsaw, and they couldn't risk giving themselves away early. He didn't check his phone in case Darren saw it, because Sam knew that even though his anger was directed at Grayson, that didn't mean it couldn't be redirected at him. Sam wanted the heist to go well—of course he did. Why would he want it to go badly? Why would he want them all to be found out and arrested, or worse? More than anything, he wanted it to go well for Darren. It had been all he could talk about in the weeks leading up to today, and he would hate to see his uncle's grand plan crumble because something went wrong—especially if Grayson did it.

 The four of them stood in a single-file line on the side of the road. Darren exhaled and looked to Vic in the truck, giving the slightest nod. Vic saw this and nodded back, then pulled off to the side and parked the truck. Darren shot a look over his shoulder that somehow got to all three of the men behind him. Sam held the rope in his right hand, Cherry with the chainsaw directly behind him, Grayson holding the shovel and bringing up the rear. Sam hoped that the others didn't know that he was the source of the rope's sudden shaking. His nerves were getting to him, but he couldn't, wouldn't, let them prevail. It was too late to pussy out now.

 "Alright," Darren said, "let's go."

 He jerked the roped as if it were a reign for a sleigh and started walking into the ditch, pulling the others along with him. Sam broke the tree line and felt a balance within him, all the worry about the heist suddenly leaving his body. He set a heavy foot into the forest and clutched onto the rope, eager for Darren to lead them all to the Giantess.

🌲

First he was there at the injured foot of the Mother herself, juvenile, a sapling among elders. It was dark, and he was scared, but trying not to be. There was nothing between him and the darkness but his barely-functional flashlight. He found nothing until there was something. A man, one that he knew, or at least recognized. The man was large, screaming because of the ants. Gary. He tried to calm him down, but he couldn't. Gary cut him with the saw. He and the Mother were alike in that way.

He shot Gary to calm him down.

Then he was at that Circle. There was another saw, not cutting the tree nor anyone. It just sat on the forest floor. He was much older now—he could feel it in his joints, his sight, his brain. They had a hard time placing him here, but they did anyway. His eyes had a hard time telling the two men before him apart from one another. The two men had a hard time understanding what to do when he said "Get down! Step away from the tree!" They went into a frenzy, one of them pulling a gun from behind them.

He shot him to calm him down.

Someone else shot the other one, but he had not been calmed. He was still upset, roaming and taking his misplaced anger along with him. He was close. Henry could feel it.

"Chief?"

"Ah, fuck! Get down!"

"What?"

"Huh?"

Henry opened his eyes, his body coming to a moment later. His arms and legs twitched erratically, scooting the chair he had been napping in against the table. The blinding florescent lights stung his vision, halos surrounding the two figures in front of him. Disoriented, the chief shifted in his chair and rubbed at his eyes, vibrant shapes flashing through the black brought on by the pressure against his eyelids. When Henry opened his eyes again, the figures were clear.

"Hank, are you okay?" Denny asked.

The name didn't sound like his, even though he knew it was to an extent. Because of his dreams, he had a hard time thinking of himself as Chief Ranger Hank Nell of Redwood National Park. Until he realized the state of his body, how it ached from not doing anything, he was fully convinced he was just Ranger Henry, barely an adult, fresh out of training, scared to even hold his revolver.

"Hank?"

"I'm fine," he finally said.

"Are you sure?" asked Vanessa. "You were mumbling during your nap."

"I didn't mean to fall asleep, I swear."

"You don't need to worry about that. You're the one that should be yelling at *us* for napping on the job."

Hank stood up from the chair. "What time is it?"

Denny checked his watch. "Seven."

"Closing already? Really?" He checked his own watch to be sure and came to the same conclusion.

"Yeah, you were out for a while. We figured we should let you sleep, you just looked so peaceful."

Hank wanted to tell them that he had in fact not been peaceful but decided against it. They were his rangers, after all, and what would they think if he told them about his past? They already knew what happened; everyone in the park and beyond knew how he became the legendary Chief Nell. But what they didn't know was that he was still plagued by the guilt of what he'd done. He wasn't a legend—he was a murderer.

But why now? Why had he put these thoughts away for most of his life only for them to creep back up in his dreams? It wasn't a rare occurrence, but Hank hadn't thought about Gary or the other two in so long. Why now did the ghosts of his past haunt him again?

He gasped out loud when he figured it out.

"Chief?" Vanessa asked. "What's up?"

"It's happening," Hank replied. "What I've feared. It's going to happen tonight."

"What?"

He was on his feet in a flash and out of the break room just as quickly. He unclipped his radio from his utility belt and thumbed around on the buttons for the emergency signal, which he pounded with such intensity that the plastic of the radio cracked a bit under the strain. After a few seconds he hit the talk button and said, "This is Chief Ranger Hank Nell. I need all rangers at the park now. This is not a drill, it's an emergency." Denny and Vanessa stood at the other side of the desk, looking at him with wide eyes. "Someone is going for the Gerschult burl," he said, releasing the talk button immediately after.

"The Giantess?" Denny asked.

"Yes. This is no longer something we can handle alone. Get the cops on the phone, tell them to set up a perimeter around the park. Be on the lookout for an old orange truck, real rust bucket." He paused and inhaled, trying to calm himself as Denny pulled out his phone and began dialing. "This clay pot's about to burst in the kiln," Hank said.

He glanced at Denny and Vanessa, both of whom looked utterly thoughtless. The chief ranger sighed and said, "Shit's about to hit the fan."

III

AFTER SHIT HITS THE FAN

13

ONE MINUTE AFTER

Grayson woke up with the worst headache he'd ever experienced. His ears were pounding with the beat of his heart, the only signal that he was actually alive. His vision was spotty and the darkness didn't help, but he could still make out his surroundings. Grayson sat up on the forest floor and looked around, expecting to see Cherry or Scrub hiding somewhere, waiting for him to come to. Instead, he saw nothing and nobody except for the space on the tree where the burl had been and a trail in the dirt leading out of the woods.

They left me? Fuck!

His ears were ringing, but he didn't know why. Maybe that's what happened when you go knocked out? Grayson clenched his jaw and forced his ears to decompress, hoping it would fix his deafness. His ears popped and he was inundated with sounds of approaching rangers that had thankfully stopped shooting toward him. Along with the footsteps, Grayson heard the dull scream of far-off police sirens. Having been pulled over for speeding and reckless driving, as well as being detained for underage drinking, it was a sound he was all too familiar with.

And he had no intention of reuniting with it.

Slowly finding his way to his feet, trying to make as little noise as possible, Grayson looked over his shoulder to see if the rangers were coming for him. He didn't find any, but heard them in his silence. He took short steps, careful to not crush any twigs beneath his feet as he crept away. He could feel his heartbeat once again, feel it in his throat. Everything sounded louder now, from his internals to the snapping and crackling on the forest floor. When the rangers' flashlights shone on the trees ahead of him, Grayson made a quick decision and bolted from his position. If he wanted to make it back to the truck, he'd have to do it fast.

Grayson made it quite a ways away before the rangers started calling to one another. He was too far away to hear what they were saying, but it didn't matter; he didn't care about what the rangers were doing. Until they started shooting.

Bullets whizzed past him and embedded into the surrounding trees, wood chips splintering from the entry wounds. Grayson picked up speed, his sides starting to burn as he darted through the woods. He wondered if the trees felt anything when they got hit, if they experienced great pain like he surely would if one of the rangers' shots actually landed. For a split second, he wished he were a tree: tall, towering, nearly indestructible, surrounded by beings just like them. Then again, if he were a tree, he couldn't run when there was trouble. And right now, he really needed to run.

Grayson followed the path that the burl carved into the ground as it was pulled out of the forest. It was easy to see since the burl was so heavy. He ran alongside the shallow canal of leaves smushed into the dirt, nearly rolling his ankle after stepping into it multiple times. The bullets had stopped flying as they were probably doing more damage than good. Grayson thought about how they were shooting at him in hopes to stop the burl thefts, but in doing so, they were actively creating more burls. *Idiots, they're making business for us*, he thought.

That was when Grayson realized he forgot to retrieve the shovel.

He almost stopped running because of the panic that slowly overtook him. Of course he forgot something! Why did it have to be the thing *he* touched? They would surely send it in to get swept for fingerprints—hell, they're probably already getting it bagged up for evidence. He was cooked! His only hope was to make it back to the truck before the rangers got him, before Vic drove away—

His ankle found a particularly low point in the trench left by the burl and promptly gave way to the side, sending Grayson tripping over himself and falling once again on the forest floor. He heard something snap when he was going down, and although it could have just been a stick, his ankle pulsed with enough pain to render him immobile. He flipped over from his stomach and sat up, facing back at where he came from and inspected his injury. There was nothing readily apparent that signaled a break, but when he tried to stand and run away, he ended up back on the ground.

The light was beginning to dim as the sun dipped out of sight. Grayson panted, trying to think up a way to crawl fast enough to get to the truck. But deep down he knew that even if he could run, he'd still come up short. He was done.

As the flashlight beams came into view, Grayson raised his hands into the air. The rangers' tan hats came into view in the late evening glow. One of them shined their flashlight directly in

Grayson's eyes, making him jerk back and squint. "Don't shoot!" he yelled. "I'm unarmed!"

"Don't move, and we won't have to shoot," one of the rangers said in a gruff tone. He approached Grayson slowly, clicking off his flashlight and holstering it in his utility belt. The ranger looked as tall as the trees around him from Grayson's perspective on the ground. "Where is it?"

"Where is what?" He really didn't know what the ranger was talking about.

"Don't be stupid! The Gerschult burl was cut from the Giantess, and we followed the trail and found you. Where the hell is the burl?" The ranger looked past Grayson at the trail that stretched on behind him.

"That way," Grayson said, pointing over his shoulder.

"Yeah, no shit."

The ranger grunted as another khaki-clad man came into view. This one was skinnier, younger than the one that first apprehended Grayson. The older one also had a badge that this one didn't. "Did you get him, chief?"

"One of them. Notify Vanessa, tell her they're headed east with the burl."

Grayson contemplated his situation for a moment, thinking about what leverage he had, if any. He knew exactly where the truck was parked, what road it was on, where it would be headed. But then he thought about Sam, his coworker, his friend. Could he really sell him out like that? Maybe he could spin the story in a way that let Sam off the hook, but still satisfied the cops. Grayson was sure he was smart enough to do that.

"I know where they're going."

The chief ranger turned back to Grayson. "Yeah, we figured. You're gonna tell us everything once the police get here."

As if on cue, the telltale sirens got louder again, sending Grayson into fight or flight mode. There was no use in the former; weren't park rangers on the same level as police officers? If he started a scuffle with them, he could get charged with assaulting law enforcement. And he couldn't run either, on account of his bum ankle. He had no choice but to comply.

But fuck, did his ankle hurt.

"Alright, get up," the chief said. "We're detaining you and escorting you to the ranger's cabin."

"I can't walk," replied Grayson. "I rolled my ankle. I think it's sprained."

"That's what you get for running from us." The chief turned to the younger, skinnier ranger who was walking up to them. "Help me with him, his ankle's sprained."

"Which one, chief?"

Grayson put his hands out in front of him and looked at the backs of them. He extended his pointer finger and thumb, then put the rest of his fingers down. After determining which of his hands formed an L shape, Grayson said, "The right one."

🌲

Vic drummed his thumbs on the steering wheel while he waited for the crew to get back. The truck was off and no music was playing, as per Darren's request of not drawing additional attention to themselves, so Vic was relying on his mental playlist, tapping out beats and rhythms to pass the time. He even started singing at one point, but stopped when he remembered what song the lyrics were from.

Our song. My song, with her.

He didn't miss her. At least, that's what he told himself—but he was wrong, of course. Vic still thought about his first date with her, when he knew that it would be more than just a couple drinks with a hookup sprinkled in somewhere. He'd had her over to watch one of his favorite movies, and they argued about the ending until three in the morning. It was supposed to be ambiguous; Ness didn't like that, and Vic did. That disagreement alone led to three more dates and four more months that they spent together.

Then Darren came along.

He'd come into the diner one day and ordered. Vic didn't know him at that point, so he just looked like a disheveled man wanting some bacon and eggs. They got to talking after Darren made it apparent that he was drunk. Vic was just trying to help him as a customer, provide as much comfort as a waiter could. Darren treated the interaction like a therapy session, dumping almost a year's worth of trauma onto Vic in a matter of minutes. He'd driven a few customers away in the process, but even so, Vic was enthralled by his story.

"My brother died a couple weeks back," Darren had told him, "and I haven't been taking it well. I tried to go to his service, and his bitch widow of a wife turned me away. Well, she didn't, but her son did. Said that if she saw me there she'd freak out." Darren shook his head and put a fist on the counter. "I told Mark so many times that he never should have married her, but he never listened to me. And look where that got him."

Darren's drunken omission of details left Vic wanting more. Was his brother dead because of his wife? Did she kill him, or did she just drive him away? Or was she so overbearing that he did it to himself? Vic didn't know, but he enjoyed the mystery. It was like those true crime shows Ness was obsessed with, but it was actually happening. To his surprise, she had no interest in Darren's story and said that the fact that he did was concerning.

"Why would you want to be invested in something like this?" Ness asked Vic. "His brother died, Victor!"

"I'm just trying to be a good person, you know, help this guy through it," Vic explained. "That's better than watching a show that makes money off of shit like this."

She was quiet after that.

Darren became a regular at the diner, but his and Vic's conversations soon steered away from tragedy and more toward their interests, what they did for work, topics one would discuss in small talk rather than a psychology study.

"I'm just here for now," said Vic. "It's enough for what I need."

Darren smirked. "You wanna make more?"

Vic leaned on the counter. "How much more?"

"More than you'll even need."

That was all Vic needed to hear. He went home that night, excited to call Ness and tell her about the new business opportunity. "It's gonna be great, babe. I just have to go into the woods and help haul downed trees out of there, or something like that. There's really nothing to it."

"Victor, are you sure you want to do this?" she asked him. "What about your diner job?"

"I'm keeping it. This new one is on a call-in basis. The guy said I'll only have to do a job with him once a month at most."

Ness was silent on the other end for a while. "So you're going to be juggling two jobs?"

"Kind of."

"When will you have time for me?"

Vic paused. "What do you mean? It'll be just like it is now."

"I know it won't," Ness said. "You'll start this new job and go off with these sketchy guys to do sketchy work out in the woods, and then you'll hang out with them just like you hang out with your diner friends."

"You don't know that."

"Yes, I do. And I'm not tolerating it."

"What?"

"We're done, Victor. I've had it. Goodbye."

He couldn't even get another word in before she hung up on him.

Distant pops brought Vic out of his flashback. He was grateful for it, because he didn't think he had the strength to stop thinking about her this time. Something about seeing her in the diner with another guy made Victor angry. Maybe it was because that guy wasn't him.

He knew that they would be back with the burl soon, or at least hoped that those pops were something other than gunshots. The most he could ask for was that the shots didn't meet their marks.

Vic sat there waiting for a while longer before he saw Darren struggling with the rope, looking like he was stringing Cherry and Scrub along with the burl at the very back end of the line. Darren made a quick waving motion at Vic, beckoning him to get out of the truck and help them. He did and almost face-planted into the ditch before finding his footing and running to grab a bit of the rope. Vic moved in between Darren and Cherry before realizing that only three of the four people who'd gone into the forest had come back. "Where's the other one?"

"Huh?" said Darren, yanking on the rope.

"The other kid, Sam's friend. Where is he?"

"Dunno. Hey, is the tailgate open?"

"No."

"Get on that."

"Darren!"

"Fuck, what?"

"Where's the kid?"

"I. Don't. Know!"

"We don't need to worry about him anymore!" Scrub shouted from the back of the rope. "Are you gonna help us pull this thing or what?"

Vic grabbed onto the rope and used the fury inside him from dredging up memories with Ness to pull the burl out of the ditch to the truck. He grabbed the chainsaw from Cherry and then ran up ahead of the crew to flip the tailgate down. "How close are they?"

"We held them for a while, but I have no idea," Scrub said as the burl wobbled on the ground below the truck. "Grayson's probably keeping them busy." Vic saw Darren throw his nephew a questioning glance before he bent down and put his hands underneath the burl.

"Fuck, it's heavy. Get down here."

The other three of them squatted and took the same position as Darren. They synchronized their breathing and heaved upwards, lifting the burl up to their knees. "Ah, shit!" Vic grunted.

"Keep lifting!" Darren yelled. They had hoisted it to their waists, and there was only a few more inches until it was above the tailgate. But Darren screamed in pain and let his side of the burl drop. It took the rest of them to lower it to the ground without the wood being damaged by the fall.

"What's up, Darren?" asked Scrub.

"My fucking shoulder," he replied. He let his injured arm fall to his side and went back down to the ground. "Lift it, come on!"

"Darren, if you're hurt—"

"Get it in the truck!"

Scrub didn't protest anymore after that. Everyone took their positions and lifted until the humongous burl was loaded into the bed of the truck. As soon as the tailgate was closed, Vic went around to the front and climbed in the driver's seat, jamming the key into the ignition and twisting until the engine turned over. He shifted into drive and gassed out onto the road, turning the steering wheel and aligning the truck in the lane.

"Oh, son of a bitch!" Cherry said from the backseat.

"What's up?" Vic looked in the rear view mirror and saw multiple sets of flashing red and blue lights. He stepped on the gas pedal a little harder.

"Guess it's time for evasive maneuvers," Darren said. "Sam, gimme my gun back."

Scrub handed the pistol up to Darren from the backseat, which caught Vic off guard. "Yo, why'd the kid have your gun?"

"Nunya. Just drive."

"Well, what do you need it for now?"

Darren rolled down his window, primed the gun, and held it loosely. "In case they get too close."

14

EIGHT MINUTES AFTER

Vanessa was surprised at how well equipped the park was in terms of transportation. She figured she would have access to the bare minimum, mountain bikes or one of the ATVs. Maybe she would have to chase down the thieves in her own vehicle, which would no doubt be the worst idea of all considering its affinity to breaking down at the worst times. Instead of all that, Chief Nell had tossed Vanessa a set of keys that he had to unclip from his utility belt. There were only two on the ring, and one of them was obviously meant to fit into the ignition of something.

"What's this for?" she asked.

"The garage attached to the cabin," the chief explained. "I would unlock it for you, but we need to move. You okay with a pursuit?"

Because Vanessa had said yes, she was staring down the meanest looking car she had ever seen. She didn't even know if it could be classified as that, thinking the name "big beefy truck thing" might suit it better. She quite literally had to climb into it, as there were no running boards and the floor of the vehicle was just under the height of her waist when she stood on the ground. The tires were huge and smelled like they were new, probably because this thing barely ever saw the light of day. After all, Vanessa had never seen it in the time she worked in the park.

That is until now, as she sat in the seat that was far too large for her to fill.

The garage door button was on the flip-down visor. The whole garage seemed to shake when Vanessa pushed the button and the heavy door slowly ascended into the ceiling. As the vehicle rumbled to life, she began checking all her mirrors and shifting things around to make it more user friendly. It was most likely user friendly to the chief, who was probably the only ranger in the park allowed or even qualified to operate this behemoth. But Vanessa would manage, and once she got the seat far enough forward so her feet touched the pedals, her confidence spiked significantly. She even smirked a little as she pulled out of the garage.

Steering out of the parking lot and onto the road, Vanessa let her foot fall all the way onto the gas pedal. The vehicle reacted by letting out a series of vrooms that were audible even inside its cabin, each one louder than the last. The sun was mostly set and the headlights turned on automatically. Vanessa was surprised at how advanced the vehicle seemed; despite its plain outside appearance, everything on the interior was controlled by a few switches or the touchscreen display. She took notice of the faint music coming from the speaker system and tapped the touchscreen a few times to see that the radio was set to the classic country station.

Yeah, that's the chief alright, Vanessa thought.

Vanessa caught a glimpse of light in her mirror and glanced up to give it more attention. When she saw that the lights were flashing red and blue, she instinctively looked down at the speedometer to check how fast she was going. She was sure that she was driving at the speed limit, at least until she got sight of the thieves. A bit of radio crackle sent her grasping at her utility belt, getting her walkie and holding it up, keeping her other hand on the steering wheel.

"Vanessa, how's she handling?" Chief Nell asked her. Then, he added, "Over."

"She? You call this thing a she?"

"Of course. Over."

"You need to fix your music taste, or at least reset the radio station before you let other people in here. And you don't need to say 'over' every time you're done talking."

The chief scoffed. "I told the police to look out for you. They should be coming up behind you any second now."

Vanessa quickly looked into her rear view mirror and saw the two police cars. "Yep, they're here."

"Good. Keep your walkie volume up. We just found one of them near the Giantess with a busted ankle."

"I'll be sure to let you know when I find the rest."

"Great. And hey, what's wrong with my taste in music?"

"Over and out." Vanessa grimaced as she hooked the walkie back on her belt and gave her full attention back to the road ahead of her. She flicked the lever on her left to turn on the high beams, which were coming in handy with the slow cover of night. Further up in the road she saw the outline of an object. It was too dark for her to make out any details, but it looked like the body of another vehicle. She couldn't rule out the possibility that it could just be someone driving home after work, but she still decided to follow them. The vehicle sped up a little, but didn't pull over to the side of the road to let the two police cars pass. It slowed down quickly and Vanessa nearly lost them as it made a turn, but managed to spin the wheel and follow them down the road as they sped off.

Not only that, but she saw that the vehicle she was pursuing was an orange truck infected with rust. And to her delight, the police cars were able to tail her around the corner.

The truck was speeding now, which was baffling considering its condition. Vanessa gassed it even more and the engine revved back at her. She could barely feel her fingers because they were wrapped so tightly around the steering wheel. The police turned on their sirens, the high-pitched wails providing the only sounds Vanessa could hear. She reached over and turned the volume dial up a little bit, the southern twang of the country music crescendoing as she did so.

One of the police cars turned on their signal and began to pass Vanessa. She let her foot off the gas for a while, allowing the cruiser to get in front of her. They were gaining on the truck, which had to be on its last leg. How could that thing be outdriving a police car? *It should have blown up by now*, Vanessa thought.

She began to hear pops ring out ahead of her. At first she brushed them off, thinking one of the many engines in her proximity was firing up because of the high speeds they were all traveling at. But then a hole suddenly appeared in her windshield, spindly cracks running through it like a spider web. Wondering if the bullets would get any closer to her, Vanessa questioned why she agreed to go out on this pursuit. Why hadn't the chief sent Denny? He would have had them by now, and he wouldn't have been half as scared as she was. Denny was courageous, and he knew his way around cars more than Vanessa. He'd driven them to all their dates, following the rules of the road the entire time. She wished he was driving and that she was in the passenger seat next to him, providing support like she always tried to do. Even if he were just on the walkie, talking her through everything, telling her it was going to be okay.

But instead of any of that, Vanessa was behind the wheel, struggling to remember which pedal she should be putting pressure on.

There were some more pops, more bullets ripping through windshields. Thankfully, none of them were going through hers anymore. The back windows of the truck were almost shot out now, the police in the car in front of her having exchanged fire. Vanessa nodded her head; it was almost over. They were almost caught, and once they were, she could go back to the cabin and see Denny and hug him tightly and never let him go. She thought about his arms around her and how good it would feel, how comfortable she'd be. She thought about looking up at him and kissing him, both of them still in their park ranger gear, having come straight from saving the day. Vanessa smiled and sighed, feeling at ease. She loosened her grip on the steering wheel enough to regain sensations in her fingers.

And then the police car in front of her hit the brakes.

She had no time to react. She tried to steer out of the way, but the cruiser lost control and turned to the left, the same way she was directing herself. Her foot switched over from the gas, but she came to an abrupt stop before she even touched the brake pedal. The sound was awful; crunching metal grinding against itself, squealing tires on the concrete road. Vanessa couldn't tell if the smoke was coming from the burning rubber or the front end of her vehicle. It was hard to determine with the airbags in her face and the windshield finally giving up, the sheet of glass peeling away from the vehicle and flopping outward.

Her ears rang and she felt like her heart was in her head with the way she felt its beating. Blood trickled down her face from an opening she couldn't feel.

It was too much for her.

Just before Vanessa blacked out, she sensed two things:

The police car behind her screeching to a halt, and the police car in front of her being engulfed in flames.

🌲

Denny set Grayson up in the break room of the cabin. There wasn't really a more accommodating place for them to stage an impromptu interrogation, but they managed. Grayson was compliant when Denny instructed him to wrap his arms around the back of the chair before locking him in place with handcuffs. "Comfy?" he asked.

"As much as I can be," Grayson replied. "I can't feel anything except my ankle. Thanks for wrapping it, by the way."

Denny sat across the table from Grayson. "I'm a ranger. I need to make sure all parkgoers are safe, whether they're here legally or not."

Grayson let out a small laugh. "You know, I don't see why you have to cuff me. It's not like I'm gonna run anywhere."

"Yeah, well, you could still do some harm if we left your arms free," said Chief Nell. He stepped up to the table on Grayson's right and leaned on it, the legs creaking under his weight. "What were you doing out there?"

"I'm not saying anything without a lawyer. I don't have to, that's my right." The kid stared forward, not making eye contact with either of the rangers.

"Yeah, that's not really how this works here." The chief leaned in even further, started tapping the table with his fingertips. "You see, Grayson, you were found running from an active crime scene. Plus, you've already told us enough to practically prove your guilt."

Grayson's eyes shifted a bit. "I haven't said anything."

Chief Nell scoffed. "So you think." He let Grayson squirm a bit more before speaking again, glanced over at Denny. "But hey, maybe we can strike a sort of deal. We don't want to put you away, but we will if we have to."

"I know you want to put me away," Grayson said. "You want to put them all away."

"Who all?" Denny asked.

Grayson was silent for a moment. "What?"

"You said that we want to put them all away. Are you talking about the others that left you behind?"

"They didn't leave me behind."

Denny cocked his head. "You're still here, though. And they aren't."

"Yeah, well..." Grayson stammered a little before giving up. It was clear to Denny that he was close to breaking. They were on the verge of getting the information they needed; just one outburst, one more slip, and they'd have them.

He wanted to press further, but the chief beat him to it. "Is this all you do, Grayson? You just go out with your buddies and cut shit off trees? Polish it up, make a coffee table?"

"I haven't even done that."

"Why not?"

Grayson opened his mouth to speak, but then smirked. "No, I see what you're getting at. You're trying to make me talk. I'm not having it, I know my rights!" It looked like he tried to cross his arms, but couldn't on account of the fact that they were shackled behind his back. Instead, he pouted and turned up his chin, averting his gaze from both Denny and Chief Nell.

But the chief wasn't done yet. "I take it this is the first job you've been on. Your little friends have been hitting trees in the area for over a year, and this is the first time we've ever caught them in the act. Well, not them. You."

Grayson blinked hard, looked from side to side a few times before setting back into his confident ignorance. Chief Nell grilled him further. "I'm not surprised at all that you were the one we caught. I can just see it radiating off of you."

"See what?" Grayson asked, almost too softly for either of the rangers to hear.

"Woe. I mean, look at the situation: you're on a mission with a group, shit goes sideways, and you're left behind. You're the classic damsel in distress."

"All you need is a dress and a dragon to guard you," Denny added.

"Fuck you," Grayson spat.

"Hey!" The chief pointed a finger. "That kind of language will land you in a much worse spot than here! I suggest you show us some respect, or we might just leave you like your comrades did."

"They didn't leave me! I fell and hit my head! They went to get help, and they were probably on their way back before you guys came a scooped me up!"

"You're lying to yourself and you know it! They forgot about you! They don't care a bag of beans for you!"

"Beans?"

"Shut up and listen! They had no intention of coming back for you. In fact, I think I heard them bickering about shooting you just so you wouldn't talk!"

"Oh, yeah? Well, I'm still here."

"They probably had piss poor aim, didn't have enough time to take a second shot. I only heard one."

"Bullshit!"

"You think they would risk getting caught for you? Do you actually believe that any of them would come back for you? They wouldn't. They didn't! You got caught, you took the fall, and they're off enjoying their spoils."

"They wouldn't do that!" Grayson's eyes were on fire, one that raged as the chief got closer, yelled louder, face reddened even more.

"You aren't worth shit to them!"

"Shut up!"

"They just needed you for muscle."

"Liar!"

"They wanted to kill you because they knew you'd talk and blow the whole thing!"

"Sam wouldn't do that!"

Aside from Grayson's heavy breathing that sounded like it might cross over to tears, the room was silent. Denny scooted back in his chair, only then realizing he had been on the edge of his seat through the full duration of the argument. He watched Chief Nell retreat slowly from Grayson, giving him some slack on the line before reeling him in even harder.

Grayson sniffed. "He wouldn't do that. He wouldn't just leave me."

"If that's the case," Nell said calmly, "then what are you still doing here?"

Grayson looked over at Denny as if he would be on his side. Denny couldn't deny that the chief had been a little hard on him, but he also knew that everything the chief had said was the truth. Instead of offering any comfort, Denny just crossed one leg over the other and stared at Grayson until he looked away. His eyes went to Chief Nell. "You suck," he said.

"Hold that thought," said the chief, placing a finger over his lips indicating for everyone to be quiet. When they were, Denny heard the wail of an ambulance siren heading toward them. The chief's brows furrowed and he turned to the door, exiting the break room and going into the main area of the cabin.

Denny got up to follow him and did his best not to look at Grayson, who was hardly in control of his emotions anymore. "Is... is that ambulance for me?" he managed to ask in between sobs. Denny didn't answer and walked swiftly out of the break room.

Chief Nell had already thrown open the door of the cabin when Denny caught up with him. He ran out onto the porch, the siren much more audible now, and only got louder as they got closer. The two rangers stood side by side and waited for the ambulance to pull into the parking lot, unload, and take Grayson away to a protected hospital.

Only this ambulance didn't slow down to do that. It flashed past the entrance to the park, lights spinning and horn blaring as it zoomed away. Denny and Nell shared a confused glance before they progressed out toward the road. The siren lessened in volume and the lights dimmed with distance. "Boy, they're trucking," said Denny.

"What more would you expect from an ambulance?" the chief replied.

Denny shrugged his shoulders. "Let's get back inside. Maybe we can get some more out of the kid before they pick him up."

Chief Nell nodded and walked back toward the cabin. Denny was about to do the same when he inhaled through his nose and smelled the slightest bit of smoke in the air.

15

Two Hours After

Based on the amount of alcohol Darren had set up, Sam thought that this party would be reminiscent of the Fourth of July. He imagined the whole house packed with people, barely enough room between everyone. If one more person showed up, there would be nowhere for them to go. People would be partying hard; Darren would make sure of that, no doubt. He would offer everyone drinks, bumps of whatever he had on hand, completely free of charge. All because of the massive hunk of wood sitting in the bed of the truck.

Instead of that party, however, it turned out that the four of them would be the only ones partying hard. Before Vic had even parked, Darren jumped out of the truck and began whooping and cheering. "Let's fucking go!" he yelled. "Best in the game!"

"Chill out, man" Cherry said. "We haven't even found a buyer yet."

"Oh, yes we have!"

Cherry slammed the truck door closed and crossed his arms. "Really?"

Darren nodded. His eyes were wide and his smile was the same, but he didn't speak while Sam and Vic got out of the truck and walked toward the house. Cherry didn't seem too interested anymore, so the subject died there and Darren followed them all into the house. That was when Sam caught sight of the bottles upon bottles of booze on the kitchen counter. "Pour yourselves a glass," Darren instructed. "You've earned it tonight."

"Don't have to tell me twice," said Vic. He swiped a bottle of rum and opened the fridge to fish out a can of cola.

"Of course Vic's still mixing his drinks," Darren said, uncapping the vodka and taking a sip straight from the bottle. He shook off the sting in his throat and said, "His little girlfriend probably taught him that."

"Fuck off, Darren."

"Hey, I'm just messing with you. Can't I do that? Shouldn't I get a pass for that, considering what we just pulled off?"

"Maybe we should all get a free pass," Vic suggested, cracking his knuckles. "Stand still and I'll try and get a good swing in."

"Guys, knock it off," Cherry interjected. "I hate having to break up your fights when you're drunk, and I like it even less when neither of you have even started drinking. Shut the hell up, don't bring up the past, and enjoy the night."

Darren was baffled by Cherry's sudden burst of confidence. "Alright, you heard him. Drink like there's no tomorrow!"

They did. Darren hoarded an entire bottle to himself while Vic and Cherry mixed each other mystery drinks. They made a game out of trying to guess what was in their glasses, and it got more difficult for them to distinguish the alcohol as the night progressed. Sam watched it all happen, lagging behind everyone and staying sober for as long as he could, faking shots and sipping on the same drink from the start. He had to keep putting more and more ice cubes in to make it look like a new, different cocktail. Eventually, it became so watered down that he could actually stomach it.

At some point during the night, the group made their way down into the basement. There, Darren dug the glass pipe out from in between the couch cushions along with a small plastic baggie. He dumped the contents of the baggie into the bulb of the pipe and then pulled his lighter out of his pants pocket.

Sam thought of Grayson as his uncle held the flame just below the bulb. He swirled the contents of his cup around as he pondered how his friend had looked sprawled out on the forest floor, how he left him there to get arrested. Of course, he was better off now than he would've been if Sam had listened to Darren. Had he really been expected to kill Grayson? What was the point? It would have only created more trouble for them, made the whole situation infinitely more sticky. Why would Darren want blood on Sam's hands?

It didn't matter. Not to Sam, at least. What mattered was that Grayson was alive when everyone thought he wasn't, and that they got the burl anyway. It was a win for all of them.

Sam hadn't known that the pipe was getting passed around until Cherry tapped him on the shoulder with it. He looked up from his cup and took the pipe and lighter, pressing the warm glass to his lips.

"Hey, are we sure he's good for that?" Vic joked. "You're not gonna barf again are you, Scrub?" He looked at Darren and laughed. Darren joined him, but not with the same intensity. Sam could tell Darren's laugh was fake and that he seemed to be getting tired of Vic, just as he'd gotten tired of Grayson. Sam hoped he wouldn't be asked to shoot him, too.

Sam inhaled and held the vapors in his lungs for a few seconds before calmly breathing them all out. He treated it like a normal breath, trying to ignore the burning sensation in his chest. But he gave in and started into a coughing fit.

"Oh, shit!" Cherry yelled. "Someone get a bucket!"

"Shut up," Sam said, still coughing. "I'm fine."

"Damn, he's a quick learner. Quicker than you, Vic."

"The hell you mean 'quicker than me'?"

Cherry threw his head back in laughter. "Oh, please. You couldn't handle smoking this shit until you insisted on buying it yourself. This is barely pure! No wonder he's choking on it so much."

"Hey, it's pure! My guy told me so."

"You really think a drug dealer is going to be honest about their product with you?"

"I paid him eighty bucks for that shit. He better have been honest."

Cherry started laughing again, hard enough to go into his own coughing fit. Sam chuckled along with him after passing the pipe back to Darren, who took it with a smile. Even Vic snickered a little bit. "Yeah, I guess I gotta find someone else to buy from now."

As the laughter died down, Sam became aware of the buzzing sound and feeling coming from his pocket. His phone was going off again and decided now was as good of a time as any to check who might be trying to contact him. Before he even unlocked his phone, Sam knew who had called him just from the twenty-eight messages they'd left. The notifications sent a chill down his spine. He tapped on the most recent one and got up from his seat, then walked to the most finished part of the basement to get out of sight from the others. Before he disappeared behind a wall, he looked at the three men lounging on the couch. They wouldn't want to hear this conversation, least of all Darren.

Sam held the phone to his ear as it rang, savoring the last few moments of calm before the line clicked and—

"Where the hell are you?"

"Mom, chill out," Sam urged.

She scoffed. "Chill out? How the hell am I supposed to chill out? Where the hell are you?"

"I'm with Grayson." He said it instinctively, his go-to fib whenever he went to Darren's house. It was more of a half-truth before tonight, because Grayson *had* always been there with him. But now, with Grayson missing in action because of Sam, it was full-blown lie. "We're just hanging out."

"Are you drinking?"

"What?"

"I asked you if you were drinking," Sam's mother repeated.

"No." Another lie. "Why would we be drinking?"

"Well, I just figured you would be, with all the alcohol you bought with my credit card."

Sam felt his face scrunch up in confusion. When would he have done that? He couldn't remember ever buying alcohol, let alone with his mother's credit card. Did she really think he would be that stupid?

Sam sighed and told the first truth of the call. "I didn't buy any alcohol, mom."

"I'm not gonna let you trick me this time, Sam! I have my statement right here!"

"Are you sure that you didn't buy it?"

His mother laughed, an actual chuckle. "It was purchased from the mini-mart, Sam. I don't go to the mini-mart. But you work there, and I can just see you swiping a case of beer when Missy isn't looking. God, you are in so much trouble! Get home right now!"

She hung up before Sam could say anything else. He took the phone away from his ear and stared down at the screen, which displayed an old picture of Sam and his parents as the wallpaper. He stood in between them, much younger and shorter than he was now, giving a smile that seemed to be missing every other tooth. Even though Sam was a child in the photo, his mother looked about the same as she did now with the exception of a few gray hairs, courtesy of her son. His father, though, looked alien to him; the last time he saw him was two weeks before the memorial service, at the funeral. It had been close family only, which meant grandparents, aunts, uncles, but no Darren.

Staring at the picture on his phone and recalling past memories, Sam realized how similar his father and his uncle were in appearance. Both of them had the same crooked nose, same incapability to grow facial hair no matter how hard they tried. When the phone screen went black and Sam saw his reflection, he found those same traits in himself. He felt heavy all of a sudden, like he swallowed a bowling ball. Unsure if he was about to repeat the events of the last time he smoked, Sam rushed to the bathroom and knelt in front of the toilet. His breathing quickened and he shut his eyes, the abrasive white light muted by his eyelids. He directed his breath through his nose, felt the dryness of his mouth and sinuses. Sam began chewing on the inside of his cheek to get some moisture into his mouth and nodded to himself, rocking and consoling his nauseated body.

Sam determined that he wasn't going to throw up. Still, he stayed there in the bathroom, not kneeling anymore but sitting with his back against the door. He held his head in both hands and willed himself not to cry. He wasn't even sure that he could, considering how dry his entire body felt at the moment.

There was a knock on the bathroom door. Sam felt it in his spine. Darren's voice came next. "Hey, you good in there, Scrub?"

Sam nodded, then realized Darren couldn't see him through the door. "Yeah," he said unconvincingly. "I'm fine. My mom just called me, I gotta get going."

"Yeah, probably for the best. It's pretty late."

Sam stood up from the floor and opened the door. Darren was on the other side of it, looking at him with a concerned expression. "You didn't puke again, did you? Man, we should stop pressing it on you. You don't have to—"

"No, I didn't puke. I'm fine. I just need to get home." He said it bluntly, not intending for it to come off as bitchy as it had. Darren didn't seem to take offense to his words, but Sam apologized to him anyway.

"No, it's alright," said Darren, clapping a hand on Sam's shoulder. "I'll drive you home."

"You sure? You've been drinking a lot tonight. Are you good to drive?"

"Good enough," replied Darren. "I've driven in worse circumstances."

"Alright. We can't take your truck, though. My mom thinks I'm with Grayson. He drove me here, and I'm pretty sure he left his keys in his car."

"Alright, let's go."

Darren stepped to the side and let Sam out of the bathroom. Still a bit disoriented, he walked over to Vic and Cherry and said goodbye for the night. He grabbed his wallet off the coffee table; he didn't remember ever taking it out of his pocket, but then again, he didn't remember much from today. Sam and Darren went up the stairs and out the front door. Sam hated the thought of using Grayson's car, or using Grayson for anything at all. Then he realized that he'd already used his friend in a lie to his mother on multiple occasions, including tonight, and that didn't make him feel any better.

Sam was indebted to Grayson; that was undeniable. But maybe, just maybe, Sam had paid him back by shooting into the sky rather than into his skull.

🌲

Denny could hardly wrap his head around all the beeping machines Vanessa was hooked up to. He had no clue what their function could be. They chirped, screamed, then subsided with no rhyme or reason. He wondered if he was the only one worried about the sounds they were making. When he stared at the IV bag, he thought he could hear it emptying. Denny scanned his eyes over the tube that ran from the bag to a needle in Vanessa's arm, losing it in the countless other tubes that were connected to other places on her body. He was no doctor, but he wondered if all that tubing was hurting her rather than helping.

At least she was cleaned up fairly well, still looked like herself. Of course, there were more scratches and stitches that hadn't been there before, but so much was expected after a crash of that caliber. When they were prepping her, trying to stabilize her, Denny kept hearing the doctors say "accident," like it was a collision at an intersection caused by an inattentive driver rather than a high-speed chase that left two members of the police force dead and Vanessa in the state she was in now. He laughed at them and how they could think something like this could happen accidentally.

Denny also heard whispers of a fire near the park, which would only add to all the calamity. One of the police cruisers had caught fire well before any emergency responders arrived at the scene. By the time the ambulance got there, the flames grew to a height of fifteen feet. The fire department came a few minutes later, and that was the last Denny chose to hear before he and Chief Nell rushed to the hospital, practically tailing Vanessa in the ambulance the entire way there.

He was alone in the room with her now; the nurse had gone to retrieve some form that required a patient's signature, as if Vanessa was able to write her name down in her condition. She wasn't even awake. Was a form really the highest priority?

Denny sat in a chair in the corner, just looking at Vanessa lying in the hospital bed. He had never been to a hospital on his own accord, only accompanied his parents whenever a loved one broke a hip or was placed into hospice care. The last time he was here, Denny watched someone very close to him die. He hoped he wouldn't have to do that tonight.

The door opened and in walked Chief Nell with an armful of bounty from the vending machine. "Took you long enough," said Denny.

"Your stupid chips got stuck," Nell explained. "I had to fight with the damn thing to get them to fall."

"You really shouldn't do that, you know. People die that way."

Chief Nell tossed Denny his chips and handed him a bottle of water. "You sound just like the nurse who walked past me," he said, ripping open a candy bar. He took a bite, then asked, "How is she?"

"I have no idea. I don't know what any of these machines do." He pointed to the one he knew to be the heart monitor. "I recognize that one, though. It hasn't flatlined yet."

"Don't say 'yet,' Oh Uh Denny. You're gonna jinx it."

"Oh, come on. How could you believe in that stuff?" Chief Nell took another bite of his bar. "What stuff?"

"Superstitions, jinxing things. Bad juju!"

"It's real, trust me."

"How can you be so sure?"

The chief wrapped up the remainder of his candy bar and set it in his lap. He chewed, looked at Denny, and swallowed. "You know the Gerschult burl?"

Denny laughed. "That's a stupid question. Of course I do, what about it?"

"I almost didn't go to the park that night. I didn't want to do anything but sleep. I could have gotten someone to cover for me, could have called in sick, said I threw up—which wasn't entirely out of the question, you know. I had gone to a pretty wild party the night before, and... well, you get it. But even through all of that, something clawed at me inside, a voice screaming at me to go into work, puke in the garbage can if I had to. I listened to that voice, of course. I couldn't ignore it. I went to work that night, and..."

"And you saved the Giantess," Denny finished.

Chief Nell shook his head. "Caught a saw in my arm is what I did. Besides, it would've taken him days to saw through that thing. Gary would've been caught by noon the next day."

"Still... If you hadn't been there, who would have taken care of things?"

"Probably one of the other rangers." Nell stared at the floor and scoffed. "One of the other rangers who couldn't care less about the park and the wildlife within it. One of the other rangers who didn't dedicate their life to protecting the forest, didn't stay with the program long enough to become a chief ranger." He looked up from the floor and turned his head toward Denny. "I wouldn't trust any of them with my responsibilities anyway," he said.

"Me neither," Denny agreed. "Not that I have as much to worry about as you."

"Heh, right." The chief unwrapped his candy bar and took another bite. Denny looked back at Vanessa in the bed, the rise and fall of her chest barely noticeable. The three of them sat in silence for a while, even though only two of them would be able to contribute to a conversation. Eventually, the chief gave another thought. "Someday you might, though."

Denny turned to Chief Nell. "What?"

"Someday you might have my responsibilities," he explained further. "I'm getting up there, you know. Retirement is looking prettier every day. But I need to make sure there's someone there to fill my shoes, and I think you're well on your way to being a chief."

"Really?"

"Really."

They fell silent again. Denny smiled to himself; did Chief Nell really just say that? Denny wasn't sure if he was being sarcastic, if this was just another one of the chief's weird mannerisms he went into from time to time. But taking into account the situation, the fact that one of his fellow rangers was laying in critical condition mere feet from them, Denny settled on the conclusion that the chief's statement was genuine. That made him feel warm inside.

The tender moment between the ranger and his apprentice was ruined by one of the machines in the room going off once again. Denny didn't think anything of it until another one of them started beeping as well, then another, and then two more. Soon a nurse rushed into the room, looking flustered. She reached over and pressed the call button, then waited impatiently for someone else to walk into the room. She pressed the button two more times before someone actually came in, a doctor who looked equally worried as the nurse, if not more. They began muttering to each other, medical jargon that Denny knew nothing about. Their conversation grew more rapid, louder as time went on, as more machines blared.

"Is everything okay?" Denny asked.

"One moment please, sir," the nurse said. She didn't even take another breath before rolling right back into her spiel. Out of all of the quick-firing words the nurse was saying, Denny was able to pick out "internal bleeding" and "emergency transfusion."

He didn't know what either of the phrases meant or what any of the machines were beeping about, but he gathered that whatever was happening with Vanessa was not good.

16

Three Hours After

The hum of the fluorescent lights was the only sound in the building. No one had come in for at least an hour, but she had stopped keeping track who knows how long ago. Still, she sat behind the counter and waited, looking longingly out the window at the empty parking lot lit by a single streetlamp. Missy was the only one in the mini-mart, and she was regretting giving Sam and Grayson off. She couldn't find anyone to cover for them, and now she was stuck working until close by herself. It wasn't unheard of, just unfortunate. And boring.

A car pulled into the parking lot a few minutes later and Missy sprang into action. She went out from behind the counter and pretended to be stocking shelves when the customer came in. Poking her head out from the end of an aisle, Missy acknowledged the woman with a smile and a nod. "Just so you know, we'll be closing in fifteen minutes," she said, using "we" as if there were more than just the two of them in the shop.

"That's alright, Missy," the woman said, "I'm just here to talk."

Missy was taken aback. Who was this lady? Did they know each other somehow? She didn't recognize her voice or her face, and she wasn't even wearing her name tag; how did she know this woman?

She poked her head out of the aisle again and looked the woman up and down, scanning her for any distinguishing features. When she found none, Missy stepped away from her charade of working and walked behind the counter to help her. "What can I do for you, ma'am?"

"I'm Sam's mom," she said. "Annie"

"Oh, of course! I thought it was you!" She didn't, but it was more polite to lie. "I thought you'd still be on vacation."

Annie looked confused. "Vacation? What vacation?"

"With Sam. He asked for a today off so you two could spend some time together."

"Did he really tell you that?" Annie put her tongue in her cheek and shook her head. "There was no vacation. I have no idea where he was tonight, but he's being driven home now. I thought you might have known what he was up to."

"Nope," Missy replied. "He's probably off with Grayson. They both asked off for today."

The woman's eyes went wide. "Yes! That's exactly it, Grayson is driving him home! Did they tell you anything?"

"Not a thing. None that were true, at least."

Annie sighed. "Well, thanks anyway. I'm going to have a long talk with him once he gets home."

"Same here," said Missy. "He works again on Monday, and I'm not sure how tough on him I should be."

"I won't be holding back." Annie turned from the counter to leave, then backtracked and asked, "Can I get a pack of menthols?"

"You sure can." Missy grabbed a pack off the wall behind her and tossed them on the counter.

"How much?"

"Don't worry, they're on the house. From one overstressed woman to another."

Annie smiled. "Thank you, Missy. Have a good night."

"You as well, take care now." Missy watched the woman leave, a bit sad that she had to return to her boredom. She checked the clock on her phone and decided that it was late enough to close. Who would need to come to a mini-mart so late at night?

Well, aside from Sam's mother. She seemed so nice; it wasn't every day that you could find someone to make small talk with. Missy had a hard time believing that a mother like Annie could produce a son like Sam. There had to be a switch-up at the hospital or something, maybe a misplaced tag or a typo on some form or chart. But then, who was she to judge a woman who had lost her husband? She couldn't imagine being a single mother was easy, let alone a single mother to a teenager. All those hormones and whatnot, making them crazy.

Missy walked to her office at the back of the store and locked the door from the outside, then made her way to the light switches and flicked them all into their off positions. As the lights' humming quieted and the store fell dark, Missy left through the front door and locked it behind her. She huffed when she got into her car, really not looking forward to the conversation she would have to have with Sam on Monday.

Just before she pulled out of the parking lot to drive home, Missy heard her phone chime from her pocket. It was the first notification she'd received in hours, and she was eager to see who was texting her. Maybe it was that cute ginger she met on that dating app, seeing if she was free for the evening. *Oh, I'll be free,* Missy thought. *As free as you need me to be.*

But it wasn't him. It was a breaking news bulletin with a headline reading "A Fire has Broken Out at Redwood National Park, Fire Department Trying to Contain It."

"Son of a bitch," Missy said, disappointed. "I need to figure out how to turn those things off."

🌲

Darren was struggling to keep his eyes open. It wasn't even eleven o'clock and he already felt like going to sleep. Normally he'd be fine and was able to stay up into the wee hours of the morning before finally crashing, but now he felt like a child trying not to fall asleep, nodding forward and jerking back into consciousness. Plus, the store where he would always get an energy drink had closed ten minutes early. He truly was shit out of luck.

His shoulder was killing him; lifting the burl today was not an easy task. He felt bad for letting Cherry and Scrub pull the brunt of its weight out of the forest, but it would have felt worse had he put as much effort in as they did. The pain was worth it, though. This was their biggest hit yet, and it would prove to be the best. It had to be, because of who they'd be selling it to. He couldn't wait to see the look on that asshole's face when—

Something trotted out onto the road, causing Darren to wake up and crank the steering wheel to swerve out of the way. He hit the brakes and regained control of the car, which wasn't even his. The car screeched to a halt fifty feet away from where the thing crossed into Darren's path. Nostrils flared, Darren swung open the car door and slammed it behind him, then walked down the road toward whatever was stupid enough to run out in front of him. He clenched his fists, felt his knuckles crack and muscles tighten. "Hey!" he called out into the night. "Get the fuck off the road! Crazy fucking creature!"

He couldn't see what was ahead of him, only silhouettes cast by the moonlight. Whatever it was scampered into the ditch and out into the woods. Darren thought about following it, beating the shit out of it for almost killing him, but decided against it and walked back to the car, cursing the thing out the whole way back. What did it think it was, jeopardizing his life like that? How stupid could something be to run out in front of a speeding object?

Darren opened the car door and sat heavily behind the wheel. Just before he reached for the gear shift, his head bobbed to the side and found a comfortable position against the passenger seat. Darren fought to stay awake, blinking hard to try and stimulate his eyes, but they became harder and harder to open each time. Eventually, they didn't open at all.

Shock. They were caught, and they had to run. No, they had to fight. It was the final stand, and nothing was going to stop Darren from pulling this off. Nothing.

He reached around behind his back and gripped the pistol tucked into his waistband. Mark watched him do this, their gazes meeting and Mark shaking his head the slightest bit. He'd already given up. His hands were in the air. He surrendered. Darren wouldn't.

He revealed the gun and aimed it at the rangers, ready to squeeze the trigger and end all of this. But the one in the front squeezed his first, and before Darren could react, Mark had jumped in front of him. He yelped in pain, scooted himself over to a tree while the blood poured from his wound. Darren looked back to the rangers, who were encroaching on them, shouting orders.

"Get on the ground!"

He would not. Darren screamed and raised his gun again, but not before the rangers open fired on him. Only one of the bullets found their mark, and even then it did a shitty job. It didn't even kill him, just hit him in the shoulder and knocked him to the ground. He went down facing Mark. He was crying. "Please. Help me."

Darren blacked out from the pain. He couldn't help him.

He woke up disoriented, the car still running but low on gas. He lifted his head from the passenger seat and looked groggily in front of him, the headlights shining on the road and nothing else. *Good*, he thought. *Nothing else is gonna run out in front of me.*

Darren shifted the car into drive and started heading back to his house. There wasn't much of the journey left, about five minutes or so. If he hadn't been disturbed by whatever ran into the road, he'd be there already. He looked out his window at the ditches around him, wondering if the thing was still out there. He thought he saw something in his rear view mirror, climbing back onto the road and staring at him in the small piece of glass, but he drove away too fast to confront it.

"Took you long enough," Vic said when Darren came back down into the basement. "What happened?"

"I almost hit something. Other than that, I was being a cautious driver. I didn't want to crash a car that wasn't even mine, much less one that belonged to someone who was murdered just a couple hours ago."

"Oh."

"I mean, think for one second about that, Vic. Would you want to be caught driving a dead man's car? Hell no!"

"I said 'oh!' Get off my ass!"

"Fuck you!" Darren flopped down on the couch next to Cherry. His eyes fell to the rug, a large spot on it where Scrub's puke had soaked in. "The kid's fine, in case either of you gave a shit."

"Did his mom see you?" asked Cherry.

"No, thankfully. I dropped him off and sped away. He practically had to tuck and roll to get out safely."

Cherry laughed and took a drink from his cup. He gulped the rest of his cocktail down, sighed, and then looked at Darren. "So who's gonna buy that big ass thing?"

Darren let a smile creep across his face. "You're not ready for it."

"Oh, yes I am." Cherry had the same expression.

"No you're not."

"Yes I am!"

"I am, too!" Vic said.

Darren looked between the two of them quickly, barely able to keep the answer to himself. "Robbie's gonna buy it!"

Cherry's excitement diminished immediately. "What? Darren, you're kidding."

"Nope! I got it all set up, all thought out."

"Robbie?" Vic thought for a moment. "The one who got you into this whole mess in the first place? You're going to sell him the Gerschult burl?"

"Hell yes I am," Darren said. "Or, at least that's what he thinks."

Cherry and Vic looked at each other, then back to Darren. "What are you saying?" Cherry asked. "Are we selling him the burl or not?"

The smile on Darren's face widened. His lips stayed together, not showing any of his teeth, his mouth stretching into a creepy grin. "Do we have any fireworks left over from the Fourth of July party?"

"Where the hell were you tonight, Sam?"

He wasn't even all the way through the door. "I told you, I was with Grayson."

"I have a hard time believing that. I thought we were supposed be on vacation."

Sam felt himself getting flustered. He'd wrapped himself up in too many lies, and now he was paying for it. He wasn't sure if he should come clean with the truth, or try to shove everything in the closet and shut the door really fast with yet another lie. There was a lump beginning to form in his throat, a pit in his stomach. "I'm sorry, mom. I'm sorry that I lied to you, and I'm sorry that I lied to Missy."

"When did you lie to me? Other than all the times in the past."

"I wasn't with Grayson tonight. Well, I was for a little while, but he…" Sam felt his eyes water, his words quivering. "I was with Darren."

His mother was stunned. "Your uncle?"

Sam nodded, the tears starting to flow.

"Why were you… What were you doing with him?"

"Look, I know you hate him, and I thought I did too. But that was just what you taught me to think. I have had more fun with him than I had with anyone at school, the most fun I've had in a while. I was actually excited to go to his Fourth of July party. I don't remember the last time I was excited for anything! I had fun, I enjoyed myself! I'm mad at myself for not trying to reach out to him sooner, for letting you control me like you have! He isn't a bad guy, mom! He's, he..."

Sam stopped when he realized his mother was crying with him. He thought this was just another overreaction, trying to make him feel bad for raising his voice at her. She covered her mouth with her hand and sat down at the kitchen table. Holding her head in her hands, she let her tears drip onto the wood. "I'm sorry," she said. Her voice shook. This was the real deal. "I'm so sorry, Sam."

He stepped toward her, sat down beside her and grabbed her hand. He rubbed the back of his mother's hand with his thumb. "It's okay," said Sam. "Mom, it's okay."

She stood up, pulling Sam up with her. They embraced each other, something that didn't happen often. He couldn't remember the last time he'd hugged his mother like this. It was probably last year, right after his father died. At least now, the hug didn't come after a traumatic event.

"He just reminds me of dad," Sam said.

"I know, I know he does," his mom said. "He reminds me of your dad, too."

Sam pulled away from his mother, his teary eyes looking into hers. They were both trying to pull themselves together, but neither were doing a good job. They laughed at that, which eased the situation and lightened the mood between them. "You're still grounded, though," his mother said. "I didn't forget about you lying to me."

"Fine," Sam said. "Then I get to spend more time with you." Normally whenever Sam got grounded, he would say that sarcastically. Now, however, he really meant it.

17

Four Hours After

She was in and out of it. She didn't know where she was or who all the people surrounding her were. Their faces were masked, a bright light shining down above them. She remembered motion, like being rolled from one place to another, but that was a while ago. She was somewhere else now. In and out of it.

There was a pain in her arm, her sense of touch the only one that wasn't overloaded. Everyone around her was chattering loudly, and she couldn't decipher any of their words—she wasn't even sure they were speaking in a language she understood. Even though the room she was in should have been clean, there was still a smell to it. Sterile. Her mouth felt the opposite, like she had metal contaminating her mouth. The taste was too much for her and she stirred on the table.

In and out of it.

One of the people noticed she was awake and quickly saw to making sure she went back to sleep. They took the mask off her face—that's what had been pinching her nose—and adjusted the straps on it before replacing it. She then felt another prick in her arm. Within seconds, she was unconscious, and as she went under, she wondered if she would ever wake up.

🌲

Denny sat in the hospital room with the chief, who was snoring in the reclining chair. Denny was on the stool under the television, which he had no idea how to operate. He checked the drawers and cabinets for a remote, but there was none to be found, and everyone outside the room was too busy saving lives to help him with his petty dilemma. There were no buttons on the TV itself, and it was therefor stuck on the channel the chief had set it to before the remote was lost: the shopping channel.

During a brief infomercial about a state-of-the-art nonstick pan, Denny closed his eyes and folded his hands in his lap. He didn't really know how to pray; he wasn't raised to go to church and never saw the draw as an adult. Even so, he did his best rendition of what a prayer might be like, running through it in his mind hoping he wasn't getting anything wrong.

Hi. I know we don't talk a lot, if at all. I know I'm gonna sound like everyone else who's found a loved one in a life-or-death situation, but you need to hear me out on this one. Vanessa's not doing great. It's weird, because she's always been strong, so much stronger than me. I don't know why she needs your help, but she does, and can't ask for it right now. I'm the best she's got, because Chief Nell is over there... Well, you know. You can see him, can't you?

Denny opened his eyes for a second, shook his head.

Sorry, got a bit off track there. But you hear me, right? You hear me?

The room remained quiet the whole time, aside from the chief's snoring. Denny looked around, wondering if he'd done a good job, hoping that Vanessa's survival wasn't dependent on his ability to pray. If it was, she'd be done for.

"I need something, man," Denny whispered out loud. "I need to know you hear me."

Just then, Chief Nell snorted loudly and shook himself awake. He blinked a few times before looking at Denny. "Time?" he asked, sleep filling his voice.

"No clue," Denny replied. "Just past ten, maybe?"

"She back yet?" The chief yawned. "Vanessa?"

"Do you see her here?"

The chief looked around for a hospital bed and, when he didn't find one, rolled over and closed his eyes again.

"You're useless," Denny said. Then he looked up at the ceiling, trying to look past it, through it, up into the sky. "Thanks for that."

After fifteen more minutes went by without word from the doctor, not as much as a little peek in the door, Denny took the opportunity to get some fresh air. He went for a walk around the hospital, going up and down the stairs rather than using the elevator to get to different floors. He found that climbing them strayed his mind away from his worries about Vanessa, the park, and the burl. His worries about the park got harder to put away by the minute, as he walked past patients, nurses, and doctors, all of them talking about the fire at Redwood National Park. He had no idea how much of it was true and how much was fabricated by bored and tired medical professionals, desperate for something new. Denny just climbed the stairs and tried to put it all out of his mind.

Thoughts of Vanessa came creeping back, though. He knew they would, but at least they were the happy ones. He remembered how she'd almost failed her ranger's exam and had to take it twice, and he helped her study for the second attempt.

"Why the hell do I have to know so many trees?" she'd asked him.

"In case a tourist asks," he replied.

"Oh, come on! No one cares about all the different tree names."

"You'd be surprised."

Vanessa aced the test the second time. That made Denny happy for two reasons: one, his hard work and tutoring skills paid off, and two, he would get to see her more often now that she'd become a ranger. He remembered a conversation they had during one of their shared breaks, about why they wanted to become rangers in the first place.

"At first, I just wanted the money," Denny had explained. "I only planned to be here for the summer, then find some other job. Of course, the chief saw right through that. When he started taking me on the burl checks... I just remember looking up, trying to see the treetops and not being able to. It was magical. I don't know what the sudden change was about, but I swear that the chief cursed me or something."

Vanessa laughed. "My reason's not that deep. I just like being outside."

"Really? That's it?"

"Yeah. That, and helping people in whatever way I can."

"And now you're helping people find the bathrooms in the park."

"Hey," Vanessa said, pointing at Denny, "if I don't, who will?" They both laughed at that for a while, then Vanessa got a solemn look on her face. "No, I mean... I tried to help somebody a while back. He was getting himself into a not-so-good situation, stretching himself too thin, and I thought... I don't know what I thought."

"What did you do?"

"I stopped talking to him, cut him off entirely. Maybe I thought that losing me was what he needed to bring him back into reality."

"How narcissistic of you," joked Denny.

"Yeah, well if it weren't for him, I would've never even thought to become a ranger."

"How did helping this guy lead to you becoming a ranger?"

Vanessa shook her head. "He wanted to take on a second job, cutting down trees and selling them or something. I don't know. It made me think of the trees, many of which I now know the names of, thanks to you."

Denny smiled at the memories and hoped he could make more with her. He knew he'd see her again, but was unsure what state it would be in. She would have to be alive; Vanessa was strong enough to make it through this, and Denny wouldn't have it any other way. He'd only been on a few dates with her—a few actual dates, at least—but Denny felt that what they had was special. Nothing like what she'd had with Victor.

When he reached the top of the staircase, Denny's mind began to wander. He'd met Victor that night in the diner and thought nothing of him. Maybe he was a nice guy, but Vanessa still broke up with him, ended things between them because of Victor's new job...

The one with the trees.

No, Denny thought. *Could it really be that simple?*

He rushed back to Vanessa's room, hoping that she'd be there and that the chief would be awake. He had to keep himself from running down the hallways, past nurses, doctors, patients, and grieving loved ones. As he turned into the doorway of the room, he prayed that he wouldn't have to join the mourners.

Denny was disappointed to see the chief still snoring in the chair and the spot where Vanessa's bed should be empty. He walked over to the chair and shook the chief awake. "Chief? Hank, you with me?"

"What? What do you want? Is she back?"

"No, not yet, but I have news."

Chief Nell sat up in the chair and met Denny's gaze. "Well, spill the beans," he said.

"I think I know who's been stealing the burls," Denny said. "It's a hunch at best, but it's a start."

"What are you waiting for? Get calling!"

"Calling who?"

"The police, firefighters, the other rangers, anyone who might have information on this guy!"

Denny looked to the floor. "The only person who knows him is in the operating room."

The chief sighed. "Look Denny, I know you're worried about her. I am too. But we have a chance to get these guys, and we can't waste it."

"I can't exactly ask her about it right now."

"No Denny, you're not thinking hard enough."

"No Hank, I am thinking hard enough. I'm thinking hard enough to know that this entire situation is fucked up, to know that my girlfriend could be dead right now. I'm not losing sight of her."

Chief Nell huffed and got out of his chair. "You know what, fine."

"Where are you going?" Denny asked before the chief could leave the room.

"Making some calls to the authorities," he said. "I'm being responsible." Before Denny could tell him off, Chief Nell added, "You just sit here and wait for her. Ask her about the guy if she's feeling good enough to talk." He left the room without another word, leaving Denny alone with that stupid shopping channel still on the TV. He went to the chair the chief had been sitting in and settled into it. As he did, he felt something poking the underside of his right thigh. He reached his hand into the crevice of the chair and pulled out a long, black piece of plastic.

"Oh, thank God," said Denny, pointing the television remote and scanning through different channels. He wanted to find something to calm his nerves until Vanessa was back in the room, but found the exact opposite being broadcast on the news channel. Denny stared at the screen with his mouth agape, watching the scene unfold. "Chief?" he called. When there was no answer, he yelled louder. "Chief! Get in here!"

Chief Nell poked his head into the doorway with his phone pressed to his ear. "Sorry, one second," he said to the person on the other end. "What? I'm on the phone here."

Denny looked at the TV and turned the volume up. The Chief came into the room and stood in the middle of it, staring at the screen with shifting eyes. He started to breathe audibly, maybe gasping, before cupping a hand over his mouth.

"What you're seeing here is live footage from Redwood National Park," reported the news anchor, "where it seems a fire has gotten a bit out of control. Authorities say there was a collision involving a ranger vehicle and two police cars, along with a pickup truck that fled the scene and is thought to have caused the crash. Two police officers have been confirmed dead and the park ranger who aided in the pursuit is currently in critical condition. Firefighters are trying to keep the flames contained to an area, but are having a hard time extinguishing them entirely. We will continue to cover this story as it progresses."

"Hey, Tommy?" Chief Nell said into his phone. "I think I'm going to have to call you back."

The room Grayson sat in now was much less welcoming than the break room at the park. Sure, the rangers were mean to him, but the dingy cinder block walls that surrounded him made him feel like he was in a prison cell. The white light hanging above him wasn't enhancing the atmosphere, either. Grayson fiddled with the chains of his handcuffs, which jingled against the metal bar that kept him at the table. The chair he sat in wasn't at all comfortable, but at least he wasn't completely bound to it like a hostage. Now, he was bound to the table like a criminal. He didn't know which was better.

The metal door squealed open and in walked an officer holding a manila folder. Grayson was worried that they pulled his file out and were about to grill him for all the little things he'd done in the past. Wasn't there an amendment for that, though? Double jeopardy or something? *No, that's a game show*, Grayson thought.

"Okay, I'll keep this one short," the officer said. "How are you feeling?"

Grayson shrugged. "My ankle still hurts, but I should be fine."

"Good, good. Now, I just got a call from the chief ranger over at Redwood National Park, and he says that one of his guys knows who took the burls."

"Okay. What does that have to do with me?"

"Well, you see, if you help us find them, maybe we'll be a little easier on your sentence. Understand?"

Grayson gulped. He was doing a pretty good job at keeping details to himself, but would he be able to keep that up? He'd already let Sam's name slip with the rangers, but how could they know who else was involved?

He didn't answer the officer, but that didn't matter. He was already sitting down on the other side of the table and opening the folder. The first thing Grayson saw was a picture, and from that moment, he knew he was screwed.

"Darren Prattiss," the officer said. "He has a record with similar stuff in the past, involved in multiple shootouts over the years including one within the park itself. Does this guy look familiar to you at all?"

Grayson stared at the photo and did his best to play dumb. He squinted at Darren's picture, looking it over for a good long while before turning his nose up at it. "Nope. Never seen him."

"Really?" The officer got a smug look on his face. "Ever come across a Sam with the same last name?"

Shit. I'm cooked. "Not sure."

"We contacted your boss at the mini-mart in town. You work with him."

"Do I? I haven't seen him there. We must be on different schedules."

"Your boss said you two work together almost exclusively."

Grayson stared blankly at the police officer, blinked a few times as he felt his mouth dry up. He cleared his throat and said, "What?"

"Grayson, I don't want to beat this information out of you, so I'm just going to tell you straight-up. Sam is Darren's nephew, and we think Darren is getting back into business. Is that true?"

A million thoughts flashed through Grayson's head at once. What would Sam think of him? Would Darren ever come back to finish the job he entrusted to Sam? What would the inside of his cell be like? Would the bed be comfortable? No, of course not. Sam was the closest thing to a friend that Grayson had, and he befriended Darren, Cherry, and Vic along with him. But were those three really his friends? They'd left him; he'd finally come to terms with that. Darren wanted him dead, but Sam let him live in spite of his uncle. Sam chose Grayson over his own family, and that had to mean something. It just had to.

"If I talk," Grayson started, "you're going to go easy on one other guy, too."

The officer scoffed. "You don't really get to make demands here."

Grayson flared his nostrils and kept his mouth closed. Although he was in handcuffs, he had power over the cops because he knew something they didn't. For the second time of the night, Grayson tried to cross his arms in defiance, but couldn't because of his restraints. His shackles got twisted and clanked against the table, so he stopped moving entirely and resorted to looking hard into the officer's eyes.

"What was that?" the officer asked him.

"That's all you're getting from me," said Grayson, "unless you promise me to leave someone out of all this."

The officer sighed and ran his tongue over the front of his teeth. He looked down at the folder on the table, whistled softly as he thumbed through the papers and reports. "We'll see," he said.

Grayson pursed his lips and took that as a win.

18

Fifteen Hours After

Darren woke up to the alarm on his phone. Normally he would regret setting an early alarm in the morning, reset it for a few hours later and go back to sleep, but today wasn't one of those days. Instead, Darren just turned off the alarm and swung his legs out from under the covers. He stretched out his back and heard his spine pop a few times before standing up, officially out of bed. The floor felt great on his feet as he strolled into the bathroom and turned on the shower faucet. Darren was eager to get ready and glad that Cherry and Vic were still sleeping; those assholes would surely find a way to ruin his joyous morning.

When the water heated up to the perfect temperature, Darren stripped to nothing and stepped into the shower. It burned a bit at first, but his skin got used to the heat after a few seconds. It was soothing to be under the water, to be cleaning himself, to be within reach of winning the poaching game. There would be a grand celebration today, and they would all be partaking. Drinking, smoking, eating whatever was in front of them, the momentous occasion concluding with the Grand Finale.

Of course, that was a ways off. Darren still needed to rinse the shampoo out of his hair.

Cherry woke up to the delightful scent of eggs and bacon wafting throughout the house. He hadn't set an alarm and was convinced his stomach woke him up, his subconscious hunger greater than his need for sleep. A good thing too, because the second he put his feet on the floor, his stomach started to rumble.

Descending the stairs, the smells hit him harder. The most pungent of them was smokey, and it reminded him of trimming trees with the chainsaw. They would always get a little burnt, or at least they would smell that way. Experiencing how different kinds of wood reacted when cut was one of Cherry's favorite things. Another one of his favorite things was breakfast. Luckily for him, he'd get both in the same twenty-four-hour period.

"Good morning, Cherry," Darren said from the stove. He used a pair of tongs to transfer the bacon from the pan to a plate lined with paper towel. "How would you like your eggs?"

"Scrambled is fine. What's all this for?"

"It's a beautiful day, is it not? The sun is already shining, birds chirping."

"You're just happy because it's a sale day."

"Not just any sale day, my friend. It's *the* sale day."

Cherry shook his head and sat down on a stool at the counter. "Whatever you say. Just load me up with some extra bacon."

🌲

Vic wasn't sure if he slept at all. He was up until at least midnight, following along with the news story about the park. The fire was humongous now; experts said it could be the biggest loss of national parkland in history. The smoke would surely worsen California's air quality, block out the sun, send some more greenhouse gases into the atmosphere. For a second, Vic wondered if he and his friends had caused the downfall of human civilization, just by stealing a chunk of wood.

He didn't really care about any of that. The only reason he kept up with the story was to see if there were any updates on the park ranger who was injured in the crash. Vic hoped it was that prick that Ness brought into the diner that one night, Danny or something. He looked like an ass. Who did he think he was, coming into Vic's place of business with his arm wrapped around a girl Vic used to love? The way she hooked her arm into his right before they left drove Vic mad. He waited all night for an update on the ranger, but got nothing. As far as he knew and hoped, they were dead. He hoped Danny was dead so he could get Ness back. She would see how weak he was, dying like a pussy, and come crawling back to him for comfort. He'd play it cool, but it would be tough not to give in. Eventually he'd let her know how he felt, though. She'd love him again, and all would be well.

Vic patted the top of his nightstand for his phone and knocked it on the floor in the process. He got out of bed and picked it up, swiped to the news app, and searched for updates on the story. The fire itself was beginning to fizzle out. *Good,* Vic thought. *No one can blame us for global warming now.* He scrolled a bit farther into the report and his eyes snapped to the words he was looking for.

To his dismay, the ranger was reported to be in stable condition.

▲

When Hank opened his eyes, he assumed he was in a dream. Denny was sitting next to the hospital bed, and Vanessa was sitting up eating some hospital meal. Both of them looked at him and smiled. "Hey, chief," Vanessa said. The only reason Hank knew he was awake was because the food Vanessa was eating looked and smelled mediocre at best.

He wanted to stand up and give Vanessa a hug, but thought against it considering she was probably fresh out of whatever operation they did on her. Instead he smiled, feeling like an idiot just sitting there. "How did it go? How are you feeling?"

"I'm fine," said Vanessa. "My arm is broken in two places, but other than that…"

"Good to hear." Hank looked to Denny. "Did you tell her yet?"

Denny nodded. "She knows where he lives, or at least his last known residence. We're thinking the rest of them are there, too. What have the police said?"

"Grayson sang like a canary. There're four others and all but one have a history with burl poaching."

"That's great news!"

"I suppose." Hank looked at the floor, closed his eyes, and sighed.

"What's that for? We're almost through with this."

"I know, and I'm happy about that. But I've dealt with these guys before, or one of them, at least."

Denny and Vanessa looked at each other before Denny's expression went grave. "Wait, is it—"

Hank held his hand up to stop Denny from finishing his thought. "Don't say it. But yes."

"I'm confused," Vanessa said. "What's going on? Who else is involved in this?"

Hank inhaled and shook his head. "The guy whose brother I killed."

▲

Sam got out of his mother's van and helped her carry the groceries into the house. He took as many as he could, the plastic bags weighing him down and their handles digging into his fingers. By the time he reached the door, his hands were numb. But it was worth it, because he didn't have to take another trip from the van to the house. Sam just had to wait for his mom, who hadn't been overzealous with her grocery load and had a free hand, to come and open the door for him.

"Help me put everything away?" his mother said.

"Of course," replied Sam. He knew it wasn't so much of a question as it was a command, but he would have agreed to help anyway. Sam forgot how much he enjoyed running errands with his mom. Something they did when his dad was alive was go shopping and then go to the closest drive-thru and eat dinner in the parking lot. Most families had a dining room table, but Sam and his parents had the middle console of a van.

They'd picked food up today, but waited until after they got home to dig in—Sam's mom bought ice cream and didn't want it to melt in the car. The greasy brown bag sat next to the mounds of gray plastic ones, emitting the enticing scent of fast food.

After he had all the groceries put away, Sam reached into his back pocket and pulled out his wallet. "Can I pay you back for lunch?"

"What? Why would you do that?" his mother asked.

"I want to start paying you back for everything I used your card for. I know you used it today, but I gotta start somewhere."

His mother sighed. "Yeah, whatever. It was only, like, eight bucks anyway."

"I think that's manageable," Sam said, opening his wallet and digging around for some cash. Only when he went to find a five and three singles, there turned out to be a lot more money than he remembered having. Most of it was twenties, and when he counted it all up, it totaled over two hundred dollars. Sam couldn't remember the last time he had more than twenty dollars in his wallet.

Then he noticed that the driver's license looked vastly different from his own. The person pictured on it, however, was all too familiar. It was his uncle Darren, looking straight forward with a closed-mouth smile.

He must've grabbed Darren's wallet by mistake last night! It was an easy enough thing to mix up; most wallets look the same, and Sam and Darren's weren't exceptions. Plus, Sam had enough of everything in his system to forget his name, so it was no wonder how he'd grabbed his uncle's wallet instead of his own.

"Hey, mom," said Sam, still holding the open wallet. "Did you know that you and Darren have the same credit card?"

His mother closed the fridge door and faced him. "Really?"

"Yeah, the same blue and everything. Come look." Sam slid the credit card out of Darren's wallet, his mom walking over and doing the same. They held the two cards side-by-side and sure enough, the colors matched perfectly.

"Wait a minute," Sam's mother said. She took Darren's card from Sam and held them close to her face, her eyes darting back and forth between the two cards. After a few moments, Sam's mother let go of both cards and they clattered to the floor. She sucked in a few breaths before finding a chair to sit down in.

"Mom, what's up?"

She didn't speak, only covered her mouth with her hand and stared at the credit cards on the floor. Sam went over to them and crouched down to inspect them. Soon enough, he realized why his mother's reaction was warranted.

The cards not only shared a common color, but also a common number, security code, and cardholder name: Mark Prattiss.

"Mom," Sam said, "both of these cards are dad's."

🌲

Waking up in a holding cell sucked ass, and despite the fact that it wasn't Grayson's first time partaking in this activity, the level of suckiness did not change. There was always too much noise for him to sleep through the night, and everyone in the station came into work super early. They all shuffled in, took their places behind desks, and started getting stuff done all before seven in the morning.

All Grayson could do was hold the shitty pillow over his head to try to block out some of the sound and fall back to sleep. That didn't happen, and his body was too awake to want to fall asleep anymore. So there he sat on the edge of the bed, listening to the police discuss how they should go about raiding and arresting Darren, Cherry, Vic, and Sam.

"We'll be assisting the rangers," the police chief said to a group of other officers. Among them was the one that Grayson talked to last night. "They've made us acutely aware that we have little jurisdiction in this case, so we'll be acting as backup only. We've been instructed to keep all suspects alive, but as always, if lethal force is necessary, use it. I'd much rather have you kill them than have them kill you.

"However, there is one suspect that we must try desperately to keep alive no matter what." Grayson watched from his cell as the chief clicked a button on the remote he was holding, which turned on a projector at the back of the room. Displayed on a white screen was Sam's face. Grayson was shocked at how recent of a photo it was and wondered how the police even got it.

"Sam Prattiss," said the chief. "Eighteen years old, nephew of suspect Darren Prattiss. According to our source, Sam doesn't live with his uncle and probably won't even be there when we raid the house. That should make keeping him alive relatively easy."

Grayson was surprised that they accepted his demand to go easy on Sam. Maybe he should have phrased it differently—"Sam doesn't get arrested, no charges go against him" or "Sam gets home safe and sound so I have someone to talk to at work next week"—but he knew this would be the most he could get by with. Of course, if Sam didn't cooperate, the agreement to go easy on him would be out the window. And if he pulled a gun...

Grayson blinked hard and tried to put his mind somewhere else. The officers filed out of the main room to start getting geared up for the raid, which only made Grayson's head spin further. What kind of heat would they be packing? Pistols? Rifles? Battering rams? Grayson's thoughts were wandering so far that he wouldn't be the slightest bit surprised if they rolled up to Darren's house in a tank. He hoped it wouldn't go that far, but hoping was all that he could do.

Hoping, and waiting on the edge of his bed for the officers to come back with Sam's head on a stake.

19

Fifteen and a Half Hours After

The call was unexpected, and the caller even more so. At least it was a quick conversation, because Robbie really didn't want to talk to this guy.

"I got something," he said. He hadn't even given a greeting.

"Who is this?"

"Darren, you bonehead."

"How the hell did you find my number? I thought I blocked you."

"Never mind that. Come by my house in an hour. You're gonna want to see what I have."

"I don't remember where you live!"

"Yes, you do," Darren said. And then he hung up.

Robbie did remember where Darren's house was. He'd just wanted to sound like he had forgotten everything about the man, their business together, but that wasn't the case and probably never would be.

When Robbie and Darren first met, they were both desperate for money. For a while, Robbie had Darren roped into a drug ring, slinging rock to whoever wanted it badly enough—and had the cash, of course. When he was giving the gist of his business model and overall income, Robbie had told Darren that meth was so profitable for three reasons: "One," Robbie explained, "it's dangerous shit to make. You ever see that show with the science teacher gone bad? He was scraping the red shit off matches just to make a batch of glass!

"Another reason is that people are just itching for it, and I mean that literally. They're desperate for the stuff, they clutch their pipes like it's the only thing keeping them alive. Half of them are willing to pay extra when supply runs low, and that's our best time for selling, because we just tell them we don't have much. Then by the time they've scratched through their skin, they slip you an extra fifty just to make the pain go away. They tweak for this shit, man. And that leads into the third reason, which is that they're so tweaked that they can't even tell if the product is shit. So most of the time, we're able to get by and make some subpar batches while selling it as the good stuff. And they never notice the difference."

Until they did. And boy, was that scary. A gaggle of angry meth heads armed with makeshift shanks and something that resembled a gun was something neither Robbie nor Darren wanted to encounter. But it happened anyway, and after that, they both left the drug ring for a brighter future.

It just so happened that the future came to them in the form of a trip, after they'd indulged in some of the product they stole before leaving the ring. On a whim, Robbie and Darren went to Redwood National Park for a tour. They stayed near the back to try and fly under the radar. Their group came to a massive tree, bigger than any they'd seen on the tour so far. "This," the tour ranger said, "is the Giantess. She's the tallest known tree in the park, just over three hundred and fifty feet tall." The ranger craned his neck to look up at the top. "Out here, we have a little story that says the Giantess is the physical incarnation of Mother Nature, standing tall and proud."

"What's that down there?" someone in the tour group asked. She pointed at the roots of the tree, above which was a large growth. To Robbie, it looked like a tumor.

"Ah, of course," said the ranger. "No part of nature is without flaw, and the mother herself is no exception. This here, ladies and gentlemen, is what's known as a burl. When a tree experiences a physically traumatic event, like a fire, lightning strike, or something eating away at it, it grows a protective shell around the affected area. It's sort of like how we get scabs on our skin after getting cut by something. But unlike our human scabs, which are pretty ugly to look at, burl wood is some of the most unique and beautiful wood out there. A lot of the decorative tables you'd see in furniture stores are made from burl wood." The ranger laughed to himself. "I can always seek one out by looking for two things: the swirly patterns in the wood, and the huge price tag attached to it."

The tour group chittered with laughter. Robbie and Darren looked at each other, and before he knew what he was doing, Robbie raised his hand from the back of the group.

"Yes, sir. What's your question?"

"Uh, how much does the wood go for?"

The ranger sighed, putting a finger to his chin and thinking. "It's a large range, you know? A lot of the more common types of burl wood costs less, of course. Some rare types go for multiple thousands depending on quality."

"How much would that go for?" Robbie pointed at the tumor-thing on the bottom of the tree, and the ranger seemed taken aback.

"Well, this burl is protected, obviously. It's illegal to cut down any and all things redwood within the park. Especially this lady right here." The ranger patted the giant tree at his side and continued talking about how everything in the park was protected under local, state, and federal law.

Robbie wasn't listening to any of that, though. He was scheming, brewing up an amazing thought while the rest of the group sat idly by. All except for Darren, who recognized immediately that Robbie was onto something. "What's up?" he asked in a hushed tone as the group began moving again.

"You remember how I told you about why we were selling meth instead of everything else?"

"Yeah. 'Cause it's super dangerous and illegal, and you can jack up the prices for that."

Robbie nodded. "I think I have an idea."

The drive to Darren's house was a simple one, requiring very few turns as a practical straight shot from Robbie's own house. Even if he wanted to forget the route, he simply wasn't stupid enough to do it.

But he was stupid enough to get in his car and start the drive. It was something he never thought he would be doing, and something he wished he wasn't doing in the moment of which he was doing it. His circular thinking was confusing him. "Son of a bitch," Robbie said to himself out loud.

Why did Darren have to call him now? He was starting to get back into the swing of things, found a good job that didn't involve angry junkies or slicing up trees, and just when he thought he was out of it, he got sucked right back in. Something about the way Darren spoke over the phone piqued Robbie's interest. Robbie was used to giving Darren orders, having been the equivalent of a superior when they were working together, but Darren had ordered him to come over and see what was up. It was odd to see the switch from follower to leader in his voice. That, and Robbie's curiosity wouldn't allow him to miss participating in this moment. He knew Darren had something, and now he needed closure. Why did Darren have to be so cryptic?

Robbie's view on the situation only got worse when he pulled into Darren's driveway. There he saw three men standing in front of the house, one with red hair, one with short blonde hair, and one with no hair at all. They all stood the exact same way, both hands in the pockets of their pants and a stoic expression on their faces. It looked so rehearsed, like they had a plan. For a moment, Robbie considered shifting into reverse and leaving. But once again, his curiosity got the better of him and he pulled off to the side of the driveway and parked the car.

He tried to remain calm—or at least appear that way—as he approached the three men. In reality, though, Robbie was shaking in his shoes with questions flying through his head. *What am I doing here? What do they want from me? What does Darren have that I would want so badly? Will it be worth it?* He hoped so, but hope was no match for reality. And the reality of the situation was that there were three men before him in the shadiest-looking stance possible.

Robbie got close enough to recognize one man out of the three, which gave him some comfort for a little while. Until he realized who the man was.

"Robbie," said Darren, stepping forward with an outstretched hand, "it's good to see you."

Robbie had to keep himself from faltering and stopping dead in his tracks. His gait suffered a bit of a scuffle in response. He clasped Darren's hand in his and shook hard, trying to keep up appearances and maintain control over the situation. "Good to see you as well."

"How have you been? It's been such a long time, what is it, two years, almost?"

What was he doing? How was Darren keeping such a cool complexion while Robbie was struggling to hold it together? "Something like that," Robbie said.

"We have a treat for you, and it's especially for you. Oh, and by 'we,' I mean my colleagues, Cherry and Vic, and myself." He pointed to the men behind him as he introduced them. They both stepped forward and shook Robbie's hand, then took their places behind Darren again. "Now, we haven't had the time to polish it up, or even make anything out of it quite yet," Darren continued, "but that, of course, will be up to you."

"Darren, what are you talking about?"

"I was hoping you'd ask. Walk with us. You remember the shed, right?" The three men started away from their positions and Robbie followed them.

"Yeah, I remember. Wait, you're still in the burl game? I figured you would've stopped after..." Robbie stopped himself, not wanting to bring up the past.

"Not at all. With all the money we made?" Darren turned to face Robbie. "We had a gold mine going! It was such easy work. That's why I was surprised when you said you wanted out."

"Well, I—"

"Yeah, yeah, I know. You had complications. You weren't sure if you were cut out for this type of thing. I understand, and I'm not asking you to come back."

Robbie was surprised. Everything Darren had been saying seemed to be leading to that exact request. "Really?"

"Yeah. Besides, we've had some great business over the past few years. Isn't that right, boys?"

"Oh yeah," the bald one, Vic, said. "Never worked a better job for a better boss."

They arrived at the shed door and Darren dug a key out of his pocket, then stuck it into the lock and twisted until there was a pop. He pushed the door open and gestured for Cherry and Vic to go in before him. Once inside the shed, Darren put his arm around Robbie's shoulder and walked him through the various tools and pieces of machinery. This was all so unlike Darren; cordiality was not something he had. Then again, Robbie hadn't seen the man in two years. But how much can a person really change? Enough to act all buddy-buddy like this?

"I've upgraded the tools since you left," Darren said. "Sprung for top-of-the-line shit, and it hasn't let me down. Produced some of the finest illegal furniture with these things." Darren laughed. "That's such a weird phrase, 'illegal furniture.' I just imagine a couch with a gun or something."

Robbie laughed through his nose, but not because he thought Darren's remark was funny. He was so put off that he didn't know what else to do but laugh.

"I hope you don't mind me showing you all this," Darren said.

"How could I," Robbie replied. "I left. Why should I be jealous of your success?"

Darren shook his head while Cherry and Vic dipped toward the back of the shed. "It's success, but it didn't come without loss."

Robbie bit his cheek. "Right. I heard about your brother when it happened. I wanted to reach out, but... you know."

"Not just Mark. Just yesterday we lost one of our crew, and I'm sure you heard about what's happening at the park."

"Yeah, real mess."

"Yeah. I hope it's worth it."

"What do you mean?"

Darren looked up at Robbie, a smirk growing from the corner of his mouth. He reached over to a panel on the wall and pressed a button, the garage door at the back of the shed grinding open. It rose into the air, midday sun pouring in from outside. The light was partially blocked by Darren's truck, something that brought Robbie great joy to see. So many awesome memories and thrilling chases in that thing. Its condition had no doubt worsened since the last time he saw it, but it had no effect on Robbie's outlook on it. He was happy that it hadn't yet fallen apart completely, but was rather still in the process of falling apart.

Cherry and Vic stood on either side of the truck, which was backed up to the garage doorway. The tailgate was closed, but Robbie could see that there was something in the truck bed, which sagged under the weight of whatever was occupying it.

"What's this?" Robbie asked.

Darren made a grand gesture at the truck. Vic and Cherry backed away from it, coming back into the shed behind Darren and Robbie. "See for yourself," Darren said.

He gave Robbie some space, inching backwards the way Cherry and Vic had. Robbie walked up to the truck and reached for the tailgate, but not before he heard a car door slam from somewhere close. He turned to face Darren, who was looking wildly from Vic to Cherry. "Darren," Robbie said, "what's up?"

"I don't know."

"Darren!"

The voice was unfamiliar to Robbie and sounded much younger than any of the men here. It was out of place. The voice called Darren's name again, louder this time.

"Is that Scrub?" Cherry asked.

"Shit, I hope not," Darren replied, taking off through the shed back to the front of the property. Vic and Cherry followed him, leaving Robbie standing at the truck.

"Yo, what? Who's Scrub? Hey!" He stood there waiting for a few more seconds before navigating back through the shed the way he came. When he emerged out the front door, he heard a loud knocking sound followed by some shouting.

"Scrub, stop it!" Vic yelled.

Robbie looked to the porch of Darren's house. On it stood a kid, no older than eighteen, pounding his fist against the front door. The kid looked out to them and stopped, then descended the porch steps.

"Sam, what are you doing here?" Darren asked.

"You have a lot of explaining to do!" the kid said. He got right up in Darren's face as he said it.

"What are you talking about? What's going on?"

"Oh, what's going on? You have no idea what's going on?"

"No! I don't! And I would love it if you'd fill me in!"

The kid didn't say anything, just looked at Darren like he wanted to kill him. In that silence, Robbie could hear the revving of engines in the distance. Everyone froze up, standing still and looking around to try and see where the sound was coming from.

"What is this, Darren?" Robbie asked. He wasn't even sure why everyone stopped moving.

"No clue."

Just then, the brief chirp of a police siren rang out through the area. That was enough to get everyone to scatter.

20

Sixteen Hours After

They were inching toward the house; Denny made sure to glance at the GPS on his phone every now and again to make sure he was still driving in the right direction.

"Pay attention to the road, Oh Uh Denny," Chief Nell said from the passenger seat. "If you make a wrong turn, I'll be sure to let you know."

"I'm just anxious," Denny replied. "Do you think this is gonna be messy?"

The chief looked out of his window. "I'd be stupid if I said no."

A few seconds of quiet were interrupted by a voice from the backseat. "Why did you stutter so much just then, chief?"

The sudden sound scared Denny enough to swerve a bit. He'd forgotten that Bennett was even there. They needed all the help they could get, and Bennett was the first and only one to volunteer for the raid.

"What was that, Ranger Bennett?" Chief Nell asked.

"You stuttered when you said Denny's name."

"No, I didn't." The chief flashed Denny a wink and a smile.

Denny smirked and turned his head back to the country road ahead of them. He almost wished Bennett hadn't tagged along purely because this wasn't his thing. Denny and Chief Nell had been chasing these poachers for such a long time, and they were finally going to catch them. It would be the perfect conclusion to the case, if it weren't for the dimwitted ranger in the back seat.

At least he kept himself busy by playing with the many switches and compartments within the car. He'd already found the lights, window controls, and the cup holders in the rear, and took it upon himself to begin exploring the front as well. He flicked a metal switch in the middle of the ceiling and was startled by the immediate sound of a police siren. Bennett quickly flicked the switch back off and averted his gaze to the floor so he wouldn't be staring directly into Chief Nell's scornful eyes.

"Are you done now?" the chief asked. Bennett nodded and folded his hands in his lap, silently electing not to move for the remainder of the ride. "We're trying to take them by surprise," the chief said. "They could've heard that and started preparing for us."

"What's the likelihood of that?" Denny asked.

"Higher than you think. If these guys have evaded us for this long, there's no telling what they might have planned."

Denny tapped his finger nervously on the steering wheel. He didn't know what kind of people they would be facing, just that they'd been stealing burls for a long time. Grayson was the only one Denny had seen face to face, and he wasn't all that intimidating—

he couldn't even tell his left from his right off the top of his head. But, then again, they probably wouldn't all be like Grayson.

Everyone breathed a shaky breath as Denny steered them into the driveway, having to idle along for a while before the house came into view. The house itself was large and beautiful, trim accentuating its corners and edges. But the lawn was a different story entirely; stones from the gravel driveway intruding into the overgrown lawn, sectioned-off flower beds devoid of life, rotten stems and fallen petals on dry mulch. If it weren't for the awful people living inside it, Denny would think the property had charm.

Two cars were parked on the side of the driveway. Denny parked the vehicle so it blocked the path, prohibiting either of the other cars from leaving easily. Chief Nell took the keys out of the ignition and clipped them to his utility belt. "Denny, check those first," he said, motioning to the cars parked beside them. "Bennett will take the house, and I'll sweep the shed."

Denny nodded and inhaled deeply before slowly opening his door and stepping out of the vehicle. While the chief did the same, Denny opened the back door for Bennett to get out of the backseat. They closed the doors with little noise and grabbed at their holsters, aiming their pistols out in front of them as they split up. Chief Nell turned his head toward Denny and gave him a nod. After Denny nodded back, they disbanded and snuck toward their targets.

His heart thudded in his chest, pulse pounding throughout his entire body as he approached the cars. Denny looked into the back window of one and saw an empty backseat with a few fast-food bags on the floor. He inched his way to the front of the car and looked in through the passenger's side. There was even less in the front seats than in the back, just a water bottle sitting in the middle console. *See? Nothing to worry about,* Denny thought as he moved on to the second car. He scanned the area for the chief or Bennett, but found neither. It would have brought him a little comfort in seeing them, but now he Denny just felt alone. His breath quickened and he started to lose his composure, eyes searching wildly for something to ground himself with. When they came up with nothing, Denny thought it best to shut them. He shook his head and massaged his temples, trying to calm himself down.

"You're going to be fine."

He heard her voice clearly, even though he knew she wasn't there. He spoke back. *"Vanessa?"*

"Hi, Denny."

"I'm scared."

"That's okay. I would be concerned if you weren't."

"What if I don't make it back from this?"

"You will. Don't you remember who trained you?"

"The chief is hard, sure, but—"

"You're going to be fine, Denny. Don't think about it too much, just go with your gut." Her voice paused for a moment. *"I'll leave you be."*

Denny opened his eyes. "Vanessa?" he said out loud. What was that? Some panic-induced hallucination? It seemed so real, like she was right there beside him, but she wasn't. He was still alone, still standing in the driveway, still holding his pistol out in front of him. Now, however, Denny was feeling much more calm.

Until he heard shuffling on the other side of the car.

Denny aimed his gun and looked in the direction of the sound, but he wasn't fast enough. In an instant, someone had tackled him to the ground, both of them landing with a grunt and the gun falling out of Denny's hand. Rough gravel stones dug into Denny's back as he struggled to get free. He grunted as his arms and legs were pinned down, immense pressure and pain on his wrists and ankles. His vision cleared, but the rage that obscured it in the first place was far from leaving his body. Especially when Denny realized who had him pinned to the ground. "You?" he asked though gritted teeth.

Victor stared down at Denny with wild eyes. "Who the fuck are you?"

"Denny, you asshole!" He wrestled against Victor's grip, but it was surprisingly strong.

Suddenly, Victor's eyes doubled in size and his mouth curved into a wicked grin. "Oh, you! The little shit Ness is with! You sure made a speedy recovery." He pressed the nails of his thumbs into Denny's wrists.

Denny winced, but as he gave in to the pain and numbness in his extremities, he also experienced a wave of confusion. "Recovery?"

Victor shifted, grabbing something out of his pocket. "That crash sure was something. Thanks to me, that is. Only other thing I could've asked for is you not making it."

"You're the one who... Do you have any idea what you've done? I wasn't the one in that truck, Vanessa was!"

Victor reeled slightly, taken aback by the news. "What?"

The break in Victor's concentration was all Denny needed to get the upper hand. He swiftly kicked his right foot behind Victor's leg and trapped it, causing Victor to collapse and roll to the side. He tried to sustain his grip on Denny's wrists, but Denny thrashed his arms and pulled himself away. Now he was on top of Victor, and he had no intention of letting him go.

Denny went for a punch, but felt a jab underneath his belly button. He looked down and watched as Victor plunged a pocket knife further into his torso. Denny yelled in pain and reached down to slap the knife away, but Victor held it tightly. All Denny did was jostle the blade inside himself, and he cried out again.

He went for the punch again, and this time he carried through. Denny's fist connected with Victor's cheek hard enough that Victor let go of the knife and Denny was able to get away. He stood up and searched for his lost gun, which was on the ground only a few feet from them. Denny lunged for it, but Victor swatted it out of Denny's reach and stood up, clutching the knife in a hand covered with Denny's blood.

"You almost killed her," Denny said.

"It should've been you," Victor spat. "And now, it will be."

Victor sliced through the air and Denny jumped back just in time before the blade cut open his stomach. He reached down and grabbed Victor's arm as it calibrated itself for another try, squeezing the wrist until Victor dropped the knife. It clattered onto the white gravel and stained the stones red.

Both of them unarmed, Denny and Victor inched closer to each other and started swinging. Denny's punches seemed to be less calculated than Victor's, catching Denny off guard. He wasn't a great fighter by any means, but how was this guy beating him? Victor was able to dodge almost every punch Denny threw at him, and Denny couldn't get out of the way of Victor's. The wound on his stomach wasn't doing any good, either. Every time Denny moved, it was like he was getting stabbed again and again in the exact same spot. Blood seeped into his tan ranger shirt as he took the punches and delivered some of his own. At one point, Denny slammed Victor's head into the door of one of the nearby cars, the white exterior spattered with red. Victor yelped and shook off the attack, throwing up his arms in defense.

Denny suddenly remembered how he'd swept Victor's leg out and thought to try it again. After blocking a punch from the left, Denny brought his leg between Victor's and tried to throw him off his balance. Victor, however, saw Denny's wide-spread legs and took the opportunity to play dirty.

Denny felt Victor's shin connect with his crotch and was hit with nausea almost instantly. His knees dipped and he fell to the ground while Victor raced over and picked up his knife off the ground. Victor stood over Denny like a wolf over a wounded rabbit before crouching down. Denny could smell the meth on Victor's breath.

"You think you can take my girl from me, huh?" Victor said. "You think you can take my girl?"

"She's not yours, you freak!"

Victor plunged the knife into Denny's side, white hot pain erupting through Denny's whole body from the one spot. He cried out until his throat began to hurt, then cried out some more as Victor twisted the knife. Denny felt it wedge deeper and deeper into his insides and worried that Victor would bore a hole into him. But Victor stopped and got up, kicked Denny in the thigh before walking away again. He returned with Denny's pistol and clicked off the safety right in front of his eyes. Denny could see right down the barrel, convinced himself he could see his reflection in the bullet that would go through his skull in just a few seconds.

"She was mine," Victor said, smiling. "And she always will be."

A shot rang out and Denny flinched, closed his eyes and jerked back so hard that he smacked his head on the gravel driveway. He was convinced that the pain was the from being shot and not the blunt-force trauma he'd given himself. He opened his eyes again just in time to see Victor stumble to the side, a horrible exit wound on the side of his face. Blood trickled over his nose as he fell over, thudding on the ground just inches away from Denny. Victor twitched while Denny freaked out and wiped the red chunks off his body. He shook, barely able to feel the pain in his side through the shock and adrenaline.

He'd just witnessed a man's head explode.

Denny's vision focused enough for him to see a figure approaching him. He began to shuffle backward, thinking it was someone else coming to finish the job Victor started. "No, get away from me! Fuck off!"

"Denny, relax! Hey, it's me, it's okay!"

Chief Nell's face was the last Denny saw before blacking out.

Robbie sprinted to the back of the shed and only ran faster when he heard another set of footsteps following him. He didn't have time to look back and see who it was, so he darted around every piece of machinery Darren had in hopes of confusing the pursuer. He made his way around the table saw before ducking underneath a shelf and balling himself up in the fetal position.

"Robbie, what the hell are you doing?"

The voice was familiar, but just barely. A pair of shoes approached Robbie's hiding spot and Cherry lowered himself to the ground. "You good?"

"Yeah, I just thought you were after me."

Cherry shook his head. "I should be. But we have bigger fish to fry." He sat down on the floor in front of Robbie.

"What do you mean? What the hell is going on here?"

Cherry shook his head. "Look, I don't know what you did to Darren, but he really fucking hates you. He told us you were the reason he started dealing, the reason he started cutting burls off trees."

"Yeah," said Robbie. "And?"

"Dude, that's messed up."

"We were living on nothing, practically starving! Do you blame us for wanting easy money?"

"I blame you for dragging him into it."

Robbie scoffed. "I bet he blew it all up, made it a bigger deal than it really was."

"I doubt it," Cherry said. "Darren said he had a plan for you, though."

"Oh, yeah? And what might that be?"

"I have no idea. That's all he would ever say. He would tell us that whenever he got drunk or high and started reminiscing. All I know is that the Gerschult burl was a part of it, so something must be going right."

Robbie rubbed his chin. "That was the thing we saw on the tree. When we first got the idea to start poaching."

"Yeah, well, all I know is it's not in the truck."

"But Darren said that it was."

"Holy shit, has no one ever lied to you?"

Robbie felt betrayed. Even though he hadn't talked to Darren in years, he still held him to high standards. He'd always treated him with respect whenever he earned it, treated him fairly in their years of business together. Why would Darren double cross him now, after so long?

Robbie looked to the truck, backed up to the opened garage door. "So, what's in there?"

Cherry just stared at the floor, not answering, eyes squinted like he was concentrating on something.

"Hey, did you hear me?"

"Shut up."

"Cherry, tell me what's—"

"Robbie, shut the fuck up!"

Cherry held a finger to his lips and Robbie stopped talking. It was faint, but he could hear the sound of a car pulling into the driveway. "Fuck," Robbie said. "Fuck, fuck, fuck."

"Shut up!"

"We're fucked! I knew I shouldn't have come!"

"Robbie, be fucking quiet!"

Robbie covered his mouth with both hands. He looked at Cherry with wide eyes, but Cherry was eerily calm. It was like there weren't truckloads of police coming to take them to jail.

Both of them flinched when they heard the car door close. It was clear that whoever was here didn't want to be heard, although they did a terrible job covering themselves. A few more seconds of silence, then some closer footsteps. Mouth still covered, Robbie locked eyes with Cherry, who was looking more scared than before. *Good,* Robbie thought. *Glad I'm not the only one.*

Robbie shut his eyes when he heard the shed door open.

"Hello?" a voice called out. "Chief ranger, Redwood National Park. Anyone here?"

Robbie opened his eyes and saw Cherry hold a finger to his lips, shaking his head.

The sound of boots on concrete echoed through the shed, off the walls of tools and machinery. As they got louder, closer, Robbie started hyperventilating. He did his best to keep the breaths silent, but it sounded like he was blowing gusts of wind with every exhale. His heartbeat was a drum, thumping from his chest and reverberating off the wall behind him, sending little vibrations out into the air that the chief ranger of Redwood National Park could most definitely hear. Across from him, Cherry shook his head, urging Robbie to stay quiet even though it seemed impossible. All Robbie wanted to do was scream. Was that a tear forming in his eye?

A sudden scream from outside almost made Robbie lose it. He had no idea who it came from, but it was enough to scare him and quicken his breathing even more. Thankfully, the boots on the floor didn't hear the breathing and retreated, the steps getting softer with distance. Robbie uncovered his mouth and stared at Cherry, who was mouthing "We're fine" over and over again.

Then there was a gunshot, and they both started to freak out.

"What the fuck is happening out there?" Robbie whispered.

"Just shut up! We'll be fine!"

Robbie looked to the truck again, at the closed tailgate. The Gerschult burl wasn't in there—but what actually was? He felt the curiosity creeping up on him, making him rise from his position underneath the shelf and going toward the truck.

"Robbie, what are you doing? Stop! Robbie, stop it! Sit back down!"

He didn't listen to Cherry. Instead, he grabbed the handle on the tailgate and slowly pulled it until there was a pop. Robbie eased the tailgate down and let go when it was completely lowered, then looked inside. He was confused and turned back to Cherry. He had a dire look on his face.

"Fireworks?" Robbie asked.

The truck bed then fizzled to life, sparks flying within it. One of the fireworks came shooting out and slammed into the shelf that Robbie had been hiding under.

"Oh, shit!" Cherry sprung up from his spot and backed away just as the firework blew, more of the small rockets following soon after. Robbie did his best to run, but was getting pelted in the back by hot, hard cardboard tubes. One of them struck the back of his head and he fell to the ground, skull pounding as the popping sounds ricocheted off the walls of the shed.

He was blinded by bright flashes of color, deafened by the small explosions, and engulfed in heat. Smoke began filling the room and Robbie found it increasingly harder to breathe. He cursed himself for breathing so many times before; if only he could have saved those for now when he really needed them.

Robbie passed out on the floor while Cherry screamed about being on fire.

🌲

Upon hearing the chirp of the police siren, Darren sprinted for the house, bursting through the front door and beginning to pace around the room. Sam was close at his heels, almost getting slammed by the door when Darren tried to close it.

"Darren, we need to talk!" Sam said.

"Yeah, okay," said Darren, still pacing. He was anything but calm. "About what?"

"About my dad."

That made Darren stop. He turned around to face Sam, his nephew's eyes filled with pain and loss at the thought of his father. Darren didn't speak, but Sam continued anyway. "Why do you have his credit card?" he asked.

Confused, Darren patted himself down, trying to feel the lump of his wallet in one of his pockets, but couldn't find it. Sam dug into his own pocket and pulled it out, then opened it and slid the blue card from its slot. "This is my dad's credit card. It's the same one my mom has, same number and everything. Why do you have it?"

"Why did you have my wallet?" Darren asked, trying to quell his temper.

"I mistook it for mine last night. I wasn't exactly in a great headspace." Sam looked at Darren accusingly. The kid was relentless.

Darren was going to have to tell him everything.

"Look," he started, "it's complicated."

"I don't care. I just want to know."

Darren closed his eyes, took a stand against the wall across from Sam. "I needed gas for the truck and forgot my wallet at home. Your dad let me use his, and I promised to pay him back eventually."

"Wait," Sam interrupted. "Why were you and my dad together? *When* were you together?"

Darren inhaled and swallowed. "On the day he died."

Sam shifted on his feet and didn't say a word. He just sat down on the sofa, his gaze not breaking from Darren's.

"We stopped at the gas station, filled up, and went to the park. I had some business to do there, and I couldn't do it on my own. It was a couple months after Robbie left me, and it was my first job back. I needed someone I could trust, someone I knew would help me. And that was your dad."

Sam glared, clenching his jaw. Darren wondered if he should keep going.

"It was routine, you know? Even easier than the job you did. At least, it was supposed to be." He stopped, massaging his brow a bit before continuing. "We were at the Ring, and the rangers found us just as we were finishing up the cut. I didn't want to go down, and I didn't want to bring your dad down with me, so I... I tried to shoot. But they shot first. Your dad jumped in front of me and took the bullet. I wanted to kill them all, shoot them down, grab your dad and run, but they got me too. In my shoulder." Darren's throat caught and he shut his eyes, feeling them well up. "He died from his injuries. I wasn't so lucky."

Tears began to stream down Darren's face. He sobbed loudly, sliding down the wall a little as snot leaked from his nose. His shoulder ached where he'd been shot, a little reminder that the pain he felt that day wasn't just emotional. His breathing became uneven, his bottom lip quivering with each pathetic intake of air. Air that his brother should be breathing instead of him.

When Darren opened his eyes, Sam had kept his calm demeanor. He was looking out the window, not showing any emotion at all—not even one shed tear trickling down his cheek. Had he heard a word Darren said?

"Sam, did—"

"They're here," Sam said.

"What?" Darren rushed over and peered out the window. A black SUV was pulling into the driveway, a symbol printed on the door. Darren didn't stick around to make sense of the symbol; he knew it was the rangers. "Sam, we need to hide."

"Fuck you!" Sam yelled.

"Go upstairs, I'm right behind you."

His nephew sat still, the same scornful look on his face.

"Sam, they're going to catch us."

"No, they're going to catch you!"

"And you're gonna be coming with me! Don't you remember? You helped me yesterday. You, Cherry, Vic, and Robbie."

"Robbie? Who's Robbie?"

"The guy buying the Gerschult burl. Well, he's not *really* buying it. That was just a cover for him to come here." Darren inhaled and remembered how today was supposed to go, how happy he would be after today was over. "We can't let them find us. Please, Sam, come with me."

He scoffed. "You think I'm gonna follow you after what you did to my father?"

"I didn't do anything to—"

"After what you did to me?"

Darren sighed. "Look Sam, I know I've been shitty to you, but let me make up for it now." He walked to the staircase, stepped onto the first stair, and looked back at Sam. He could hear the closing of car doors coming from outside. "Come on."

Sam got up and walked to Darren, their eyes meeting at the same level. Darren was surprised at how big Sam was. He'd always remembered him as the little shit running around, pooping his pants and smiling while he did it. Now, Sam looked just like his dad. Darren could see Mark in his nephew's eyes, his hair and the way it curled, his broad shoulders that hosted little muscle. Darren felt himself start to go in for a hug, but then Sam spoke.

"I'm not going anywhere with you."

Then there was a voice at the door. "Redwood National Park. Anyone home?"

Darren's eyes went wide. Sam's eyes narrowed at Darren, and in one swift motion lunged for the door and threw back the deadbolt. Just as he was about to twist the handle, Darren grabbed Sam's other hand and yanked him toward the stairway. The front door opened, but Darren had already begun shoving Sam up the stairs and couldn't divert his attention to deal with it. Instead, he hustled up after Sam and stopped halfway up the steps, turning around and facing whatever scummy ranger was breaking into the house.

"Redwood National Park!" the voice said again. The ranger was on the other side of the stairwell, barely in the house. "Stand down! Unarm yourself and surrender, now!"

A few moments of silence passed, Sam and Darren both stopped on the stairs. Neither of them made a sound.

"If you put up a fight, I will resort to lethal force."

Darren looked over his shoulder at Sam. There wasn't a lick of fear in his nephew's eyes. And even though Darren was scared out of his mind, he clenched his jaw and hardened his gaze, looking at the wall like he could see the ranger on the other side.

"If you shoot me," Darren said, "you're going to have all hell to pay."

The ranger spun around the wall and stood at the bottom of the staircase, aiming his pistol in front of him. When he started coming up the steps, Darren set himself two steps above the ranger. From there, he raised one of his legs and kicked his foot out, the sole connecting with the ranger's sternum and sending him into the wall at the bottom of the staircase. The ranger grunted as his head slammed into the wall; Darren couldn't tell if the cracking sound came from the broken drywall or the ranger's skull. Either way, he watched the ranger fall to the floor, his pistol having flung from his hands and landing out of sight.

Darren and Sam stood, huffing out panicked breaths as they stared down at the immobile ranger on the floor. "Did you kill him?" Sam asked.

"I don't know," Darren replied, "but I don't think we should stay here to find out."

"Okay, great. I'm going outside to turn you in." Sam took one step down the stairs and Darren threw his arms out to the side, blocking the path. "Darren, let me through!"

"No! We can still fight this!"

Sam struggled against Darren's hold. "You're done! Just let me go home!"

"I can't! I won't! I—"

A series of pops rattled off outside. Though muffled by the walls of the house, Darren knew exactly what had happened.

"What the hell is that?" Sam asked.

"No," Darren said. "It's the Grand Finale."

Sam stopped pressing against Darren's arms. "What?"

"I had the truck rigged with leftover fireworks from the Fourth of July party. Big mean ones. Robbie was supposed to open the tailgate and get blasted by them, payback for the shit he brought down on me."

"You're insane!" Sam pushed hard on Darren's back and managed to slip past him, quickly descending the stairs and stepping over the fallen ranger. Darren tried to swipe a hand out and catch Sam by the collar of his shirt, but he couldn't quite reach. He had no choice but to chase out after him before he did something stupid. By the time he got to him, it was already too late.

"Rangers, he's in the house!" Sam called, waving his arms above his head. Darren couldn't see anybody except a guy on the ground, dressed the same as the ranger in the house. He was bleeding from his stomach. Darren's eyes moved to the figure next to the ranger and was filled with nausea.

Vic's lifeless body lay limp next to Robbie's car, his blood splattered all over the gravel. Darren had to cover his mouth to keep from throwing up. Sam kept on yelling, not caring at all about the dead body mere feet away from him. Eventually, someone poked their head out of the shed door. When they stepped completely out, Darren could see that it was another ranger in his stupid khaki uniform. As he ducked down to stay out of sight, he realized something about this ranger was familiar. He was pretty far away, but Darren could make out the makeup of the ranger's face. And as he remembered who this was, his shoulder began to ache.

"Ranger!" Sam called. "He's in the house!"

The chief raised his pistol and aimed it at Sam. "Keep your hands still! Get down on the ground!"

Sam did as the ranger said. Something about the scene—Sam kneeling on the ground, at the mercy of the man who killed his father—lit a fire inside Darren. He could feel the heat in his chest, rising and building, hearing the steam hiss out of his ears. What was he doing here, cowering inside, while his nephew, his blood, was being detained? Is this what Darren wanted?

No.

Darren burst out from the doorway, pounding feet carrying him across the gravel in a flash. He flew by Sam and kept barreling toward the chief ranger, who was adjusting his aim to fire a shot at Darren. A bullet caught him in the leg, just below his left hip, but he was going too fast to stop. Darren tackled the ranger to the ground, seeming to fly through the air with him before they landed. There was a frightened look on the ranger's face, one that Darren relished seeing. The chief coughed and wheezed, the wind having been knocked out of him in the fall. He was so vulnerable, such a smear of shit—in this moment, Darren saw him as just that.

The ranger's face grew smug as he regained his breath. Darren felt the ranger's lungs rise and fall beneath his own. He wanted nothing more than to make them stop, and he decided that he would do his best to try.

Darren lifted his hand above his head and squeezed it into a fist, then brought his knuckles down hard on the chief's face. Blood leaked down his nose, dripped off of Darren's hand as he brought it back up for another punch. "You killed my fucking brother!" he yelled. His fist connected hard with the chief's cheek and he thought he heard something break, so Darren went for the same spot again for good measure. When the chief cried out in pain, Darren knew he'd done the job.

"Stop! Get off the chief!"

Darren didn't stop despite the other ranger's pleas. How'd that fucker get up anyway? He was knocked out cold when Darren kicked him into the wall, and now he was trying to order him around? Darren actually laughed out loud when he thought about it.

"Darren, stop!" Sam cried. "Darren, get off him!"

"Get on the ground, now!"

One more punch. *One more.*

Just as he was about to deliver a nose-breaking blow, Darren's hand was restrained. He spun around, expecting to see the pansy-ass ranger that he'd kicked the shit out of, but instead saw Sam. He wrestled his arm out of Sam's grasp. "Sam, get out of here."

"No. You need to stop!"

"Hey, kid!" the ranger shouted, raising his pistol a little. "Get away from them!"

"Sam, you gotta go, now."

"No!"

"Kid, get the fuck out of the way! I need to fire!"

"Sam! Go!" Darren looked past his nephew and saw the ranger lifting the gun up to shoot. "No!"

As the pop rang out, Darren shoved Sam behind him and he landed on top of the broken and bloody chief. The ranger stood with a smoking gun, staring at the scene before him. He ran over to the pile of people, pulling everyone away from each other and separating them by a few feet. Darren was first, put in handcuffs almost immediately. But as the ranger moved on to Sam and the chief, Darren began to feel a sharp pain in his lower chest. Looking down, he saw a hole in his shirt that was slowly turning red.

"Oh, shit."

Sam looked over at Darren. "Hey, he's shot!"

Darren coughed and the pain worsened, going from a small pang to indescribable anguish. He felt someone rush to his side, beginning to assess the wound. Darren blinked once and saw him there.

"Mark?"

His brother was smiling at him with thankful eyes.

Darren blinked again and he was gone. He closed his eyes and fell into darkness.

21

Eighteen Hours After

Denny could hear a familiar beeping sound, smelled that familiar sterile scent, but could see nothing. He was in the hospital, of course; that meant he'd survived the raid. But what about Chief Nell and Bennett? Were they here, too? Or were they being shipped to the nearest mortuary to get their body pumped and mouths wired shut? Denny started to panic, and the beeping on the machine got faster, more erratic. That's when he realized he was the one hooked up to it, and when he felt the hospital mattress beneath him, the thin blanket covering his body, and the needle in his arm. But why couldn't he see anything?

Slowly, his eyes blinked open and he was blinded by the harsh fluorescent lights. Denny had to squint to keep from getting disoriented, but the shapes around him began to sharpen into objects. There was the white blanket, the gray frame of the bed, the blue privacy curtains on either side of him. But where was everyone else?

Though they had adjusted to the light, Denny's eyes could only open halfway—probably something to do with how foggy his brain was feeling. How long had he been out? An hour or two? Days? Weeks? Denny had no idea and couldn't even begin to form one. He was too tired to think.

Suddenly, the privacy curtain on his right was ripped open, the squeal of rings on the metal bar jolting Denny into a more attentive state. The beeping machine sped up again, then slowed down gradually as the blurry nurse spoke to him.

"Hey, glad to see you're awake! How are you feeling?"

Denny shifted his head to look at the nurse, meeting what he thought were her eyes—he truly couldn't tell. "Wha... What ha..."

"On a scale of one to ten, how are you doing?"

Denny coughed and felt a terrible stab under his belly button and in his side. He groaned and licked his dry lips with a sandpaper tongue. "Two."

"Hmm, okay," the nurse said. "We always hope for a high number there, but we can't always make it happen. Is there anything I can get you that would make you feel better?"

It felt like the knife was still inside him. Was it? Did they have to stab him again to keep it from bleeding? "Water."

"Great, I'll be right back."

The nurse turned around and pulled back the privacy curtain. As Denny listened to her footsteps retreat, he felt sleepy again. He fought to keep his eyes open, blinking heavily multiple times before allowing himself to fall asleep.

When Denny opened his eyes again, he could open them all the way. Whatever meds they'd given him must've worn off, or he had gotten used to them. He didn't know or care how medicine worked, but was thankful that it did. If it didn't, then he would probably be feeling a whole lot worse right now. Maybe even a one on the nurse's scale.

This time when he woke up, the machine didn't beep like crazy and remained at a steady beat. His eyes weren't stinging as much as the first time, either. Denny found he had more mobility as well, able to move his arms underneath the blanket and wiggle his toes, which seemed so far away. He smacked his lips and rested his head back on the pillow, turning to the side and looking at his bedside table. Sitting on it was a small paper cup, which Denny reached for in a heartbeat and downed the contents in two. He was actually able to keep track, thanks to the incessant beeping of the machine.

The privacy curtain was yanked once again, the sound not as grating this time around. The nurse, a welcoming smile on her face, glanced back and forth between Denny and the empty cup in his hand. "Wow, someone was thirsty!"

"Yeah."

"Feeling any better? One to ten?"

"About a four now. I'm conscious." The first time she asked, Denny couldn't even give her complete sentences.

"Great, that's more like it! Would you like a refill?"

Denny smiled. "Yes, please."

"Wonderful, I'll be right back."

The nurse pulled the privacy curtain and was about to walk away, but Denny stopped her before she could leave. "Hey, nurse...?"

"Nurse Tracy," she said. "What can I do for you?"

"Has anyone else come in today?"

Tracy thought for a moment. "Plenty of people have come in, yes."

Denny laughed and shook his head. "No, sorry. I mean, has anyone else come in from the… incident I was involved in."

"I'm not sure, dear. I wasn't given a lot of details, but I can sure look someone up for you if you have their name."

"Hank Nell," said Denny. "Oh, and Vanessa Barnes."

"Sure thing, I'll be back in a few."

Tracy turned to leave once more, but something jumped into Denny's brain just before she was gone. "Oh, Nurse Tracy?" She turned, somehow still keeping a pleasant composure even after being called back a second time. "Sorry. Do you happen to have any information of the fire at the park?"

"Oh, at Redwood?"

Denny nodded.

"I didn't know there was a fire there, dear. I'm sure it would be on the news, though. Should I put it on?"

"If it wouldn't be too much trouble."

"None at all," Tracy said with a smile. She went over to the desk and found the remote for the TV and turned it on. She clicked a button a few times until the TV was set to the news channel. "Now, the volume is muted, but there are captions. Will that be okay?"

"Yes, of course. Thank you."

"No problem. I'll be back with your water soon."

After Tracy disappeared behind the privacy curtain, Denny focused his eyes on the TV. There was a breaking news bulletin flashing across the screen. Denny read the words appearing on the screen as the news anchor spoke them:

"We are just now getting reports of a raid involving three Redwood National Park rangers. The rangers went to a house about an hour away from the park to retrieve stolen redwood. The thieves broke into the park and cut burls, or beautiful growths, from the trees, which they will then craft into novelty furniture and sell under the radar for thousands of dollars. The raid was conducted earlier today under watch of Hank Nell, the chief ranger at Redwood National Park.

"We have Martin live out in the field, or rather on the property at which the raid took place. Martin, what have you got?"

Another image of a reporter standing outside came up beside the main anchor. Denny could recognize the house behind the reporter, the one he nearly died at just hours ago. Only now, it was swarming with police, some walking across the background. *What happened after I passed out?* Denny thought.

"Yeah, Will," the reporter said, "there's not a whole lot of information at this point, but thankfully we have someone here who might be able to clear some things up." The camera panned from the reporter to someone Denny was shocked to see was still alive. "Here we have Bennett Hutch, one of the rangers who assisted Chief Nell in the raid. Bennett, what's the story?"

"Pretty cut and dry, you know?" said Bennett, hands on his hips. "We came in, split up. I went into the house and found two of them on the stairway, told them to come quietly, you know? They weren't compliant, evaded me for a while before I came out to the front lawn and arrested them."

Denny scoffed. How the hell did Bennett make it on the news? Denny didn't believe a word he said, but some of it had to be true considering the police were there.

"How many thieves were there, Bennett?"

"Five total. One of them has been in custody since the incident occurred and has been a great help in identifying the others involved. Four of them were here today, along with another man we suspect was here to buy the burl from the thieves."

"Have you found the burl yet?"

"No, we're still searching the premises."

"And where are the other two rangers?"

"At the hospital, being treated for their injuries. One was stabbed twice in the abdomen, and the chief was beat pretty badly."

"Any word on how they're doing?"

Bennett shook his head. "The last I saw, they were being loaded into an ambulance. They were alive then, so I guess we can only hope they stay that way."

"Right, we can only hope. Thank you, Bennett, we'll let you get back to it." As the reporter addressed the camera, Bennett walked out of frame toward the house. "There you have it, Will, straight from Bennett Hutch. Back to you."

"Thanks there, Martin," said the news anchor. "We'll be following this story and updating you all live as it unfolds."

The privacy curtain moved and revealed Tracy on the other side. She held a new cup of water and a happy gaze. "So," she said, "I checked out both the names, and they're both in stable condition. Hank did have a few broken bones in his face, though, might have to do some reconstructive surgery. Other than that, they're fine."

Denny sighed heavily, so relieved he felt like he might cry. He quelled his emotions by drinking the water, filling his mouth and keeping it there for a few moments, letting the cool liquid chill the inside of his cheeks before swallowing it. Vanessa was still stable. The chief was alive. "Thank you, Tracy."

"Of course. How are we feeling now?"

Denny closed his eyes and breathed deeply. "Ten."

Denny was going insane over not being able to hear any sound from the TV. Another patient woke up and requested that the channel be changed to some reality show about rich people living on the coast.

Denny didn't know how anyone could tell all the reality shows apart; weren't they all about rich people living on the coast?

Eventually, Tracy returned and said that he was stable enough to be moved into a recovery room until he was released. "Unless something goes wrong, you won't have to stay overnight" said Tracy as she wheeled him through the hospital. "Isn't that fantastic?"

"It sure is, Tracy," Denny said, doing his best to match her energy.

"And you even have a visitor!"

"What? I do?"

They stopped in front of an open doorway, an empty room on the other side of it. Empty, except for the woman sitting in a wheelchair in the corner. Denny couldn't have asked for a better person to see.

"Vanessa," he said as Tracy positioned and adjusted his bed.

"Hi," greeted Vanessa.

"I'll let you two be," Tracy said. "Press the call button if you need absolutely anything."

"Thank you, Tracy." Denny waited until the door closed behind her to speak again. "How are you feeling?"

Vanessa chuckled. "On a scale of one to ten? Eight."

Denny nodded. "Nice. Have you seen the chief yet?"

"No, you?"

"Nope. But I heard from the nurse that he's stable. They messed up his face, apparently."

"I didn't think they could mess it up any worse than it already was."

Denny laughed. "Yeah, I hear that." He exhaled and pursed his lips, wondering if he should really say what he was about to. "Your ex boyfriend stabbed me."

Vanessa's brow furrowed. "Victor?"

"Yeah."

"Huh. I never pinned him as the violent type."

"Well, I can tell you from experience that he is. Got the scars to prove it and everything."

"I'm sorry that you got involved with that. I shouldn't have brought you to that diner. I honestly didn't even know he was working that night, but I shouldn't have even taken the chance."

"Why did you take me there?"

Vanessa shrugged. "I guess I just wanted to rub it in his face. Rub *you* in his face."

Denny grimaced. "Ew, I don't like how you phrased that."

Vanessa snorted. "You know what I mean. I wanted him to know that I've moved on. Apparently he didn't get the message. We might have to go back to the diner together and let him know again."

As Vanessa laughed at her own joke, Denny struggled to hold eye contact with her. She didn't know that Chief Nell killed Victor. He thought about telling her, but the way she was smiling told him that he should keep his mouth shut. Wait for the chief to mention it, if he even remembered. For now, though, Denny just wanted to see Vanessa happy. He missed seeing her smile, the way her face scrunched up when she laughed, everything about her. At the moment, Denny was feeling eleven, at least.

The door opened and a nurse that wasn't Tracy walked into the room. "Hello, are you two Denny and Vanessa?"

"Yeah," they said together.

"I'm Blake, the nurse keeping an eye on Hank."

Denny braced himself for bad news in the second the nurse paused for a breath.

"He has a message for the both of you."

Vanessa and Denny shared a confused glance. "What do you mean?" Vanessa asked. "Is he alright? Why wouldn't he just tell us himself?"

"That's the issue. Hank is fine, but in really rough shape. His entire face is bruised and he barely speaks because the pain medication he was prescribed numbed so much. He just doesn't want you two to see him right now in that condition."

Vanessa sighed. "Of course not."

"But he's okay?" Denny asked. "Everything's okay with him? He won't die?"

A slight grin crept onto Blake's face. "No, he won't die. He's going to be just fine, one his face heals."

Denny nodded. "Great. Thank you for letting us know."

"Of course." Blake grabbed the door handle and left the room. After the door clicked closed, Denny could hear Vanessa laughing to herself.

"What?"

She stopped and looked at him. "I never thought he would be so vain. 'Oh, I don't want my rangers to see me without my beauty rest!' Give me a break."

Denny cracked, erupting into laughter that made his stomach-ache terribly. He didn't care, though. He was here, and she was there, and that's all he could ask for.

▲

An officer led Sam to a door while holding the chain of Sam's handcuffs. The added strain made the metal dig into Sam's wrists, made his hands start to go numb. The officer reached over and twisted the knob, then pushed the door open. As it swung into the room, Sam took notice of the sparse contents of the room: a metal table, two chairs, and Grayson sitting in the one furthest from the door. Sam wasn't all that surprised to see him, though when he was told he had a visitor, he was hoping it was Darren. He didn't want to talk to him, but he just wanted to know he was alive. Then, one way or another, Darren would pay for everything he did.

The officer closed and locked the door before unlocking Sam's restraints, his wrists instantly relieved of pain as blood flowed once again into his hands. The officer then sat Sam down at the table and ran the handcuffs under a bar, hooking them back onto Sam and exiting the room without saying a word. As Sam stared down at the table, he could feel Grayson looking at him. After a few moments of silence, Sam looked up and met Grayson's gaze. He didn't seem mad about the situation, as Sam had expected him to be. Instead, he looked content, almost grateful. When he spoke, Sam realized why.

"Thank you for not killing me."

"Thank you for getting them to let me off easy. Or, as easy as they could."

"Yeah." Grayson shrugged. "Two months isn't so bad. I heard Cherry's getting upwards of twenty years, and that's just for cutting the trees. Not to mention all the drugs and everything with Darren."

"What did they decide for you?" Sam asked.

"Four months probation, because I gave them information. Plus, I didn't kill anybody. Even though that's, like, the bare minimum."

Sam laughed. "Tell me about it."

"Yeah. Thanks again."

The air between them went silent. Sam shifted a little, his chain rattling against the table.

"Has your mom come to see you yet?" asked Grayson.

"No, but she called," Sam replied. "She's pissed, of course. She might actually kick me out of the house this time."

"Ah, come on. She's made that threat before."

"I don't know. She sounded serious."

"Well, if she is, you're welcome to come and live with me." Grayson cocked his head and smirked, as if he deserved a prize for the gracious offering.

"I'll keep that in mind."

"Yeah, just let me know whenever we have a shift together."

Sam pursed his lips. "Pretty sure we're fired, Grayson."

"Huh? Why... Oh."

"Yeah."

"Shit."

"We'll figure something out. We've got a while before we have to worry about it."

"Right." Grayson's expression went somber, and Sam could feel his own following suit. He always thought of himself as a pretty okay person; by no means the best, but definitely not the worst. At the time, he thought getting expelled was the worst thing to happen to him. Now, there was something infinitely worse. What would happen while he was in jail? What would happen once he got out? Would people know about him, what he'd done, who he did it with? Or would they not even care and pass him by without a second glance? Sam didn't know which scenario was worse.

He thought back to the day he got expelled, how awful he felt. It wasn't so much regret—after all, Cory *was* an asshole. He felt shameful, especially when he had to give his mother the letter the superintendent wrote. All Sam could do was slide it across the kitchen table, hang his head, and wait for her to blow up at him.

Then, Sam realized that he got expelled two months ago. Had it really been that long already? It was the same amount of time he was to be imprisoned for, after which he would have to do some community service and pay a fine. It eased him to know that it would be over in no time. He wondered if he might see Darren on the inside, wondered if he would get the chance to stick a shiv in his side in the courtyard. "Hey, how much time did everyone else get?"

Grayson swallowed. "What do you mean?"

Sam narrowed his eyes. "Are you kidding? You said that Cherry was getting over twenty years. How much time did Darren get?"

Grayson glanced down at the table, eyes fluttering across the metal surface. Sam watched him form a response in his mind, could practically see the gears turning, smoke billowing from the top of his head. "Darren died, Sam."

Sam scoffed. "Good one." He entered a fit of nervous laughter, shaking his head and shutting his eyes. But when he opened them, Grayson wasn't laughing. He didn't even have a smile on his face. "What are you looking at me like that for?"

"I'm really sorry that I have to be the one to tell you this. I figured they would have mentioned it already, some sick psychological torture or whatever."

"Grayson, what are you talking about?"

Grayson sighed. "Darren was shot in the chest, and the bullet hit something near his heart. It stopped before they even got to the hospital."

Sam was speechless. "But, the people in the ambulance, they didn't help him?"

"I'm sure they did, but—"

"They didn't help him because he's a bad guy? Is that what happened?"

"Sam, I don't think—"

Sam stood up, his chair scraping against the concrete floor before toppling over. "That's horseshit! Why would they do that? Why would they just let him die?" His handcuffs rattled with every word. He heard the door unlock behind him, an officer rushing in to assess the situation.

Grayson stood up as well, putting both his hands up and trying to calm Sam down. "They didn't let him die."

"Yes, they did! They let him die because he… he was…"

He lost his train of thought as the officer forced Sam back into his seat. "Control yourself," the officer said, "or I'm gonna have to call this early."

"Call it," Sam said. "Take me out of here."

Grayson shook his head. "Sam, I'm sorry."

"Whatever." He looked to the officer. "I'm ready to leave."

While his cuffs were switched, Sam mulled over Darren's death. Why had he reacted like that? It was the anger, because now Darren couldn't be punished for stealing the credit card, for leading Sam's dad to his death, and nearly leading Sam to the same fate. He wouldn't have to sit and rot in a cell for the rest of his life, wishing every day that he could go back and change what he did, the choices he made. Now, Darren was just dead, leaving Sam with the memories of it all.

But was that really the only reason? Or was it also that, because Darren was dead, Sam now had no ties to his father? Darren had been the only other person on his dad's side that was still alive, and now he was gone. Now, Sam's father was truly gone.

Sam looked back at Grayson before the officer shoved him out of the room. "I'm glad I didn't shoot you," he said. Sam could see Grayson smile before the door closed behind him.

22

Two Months After

As the fall season rolled in and temperatures dipped once again, Denny found himself working the desk at the ranger's cabin. He'd just helped a couple find their way to the Grove, where they would be taking their engagement photos. "That's a fine choice of a spot if I ever heard one," Denny said. "Make sure to tag the park's page if you end up posting them on social media. We'd love to see them."

The couple gave Denny their thanks and giggled excitedly to each other while they walked out the door. Denny smiled as he went back to leaning on one fist as he pretended to do work on the computer in front of him. After clicking the mouse a few times, the door to the cabin opened. He typed random letters into an empty document as he went into greeting mode. "Welcome to Redwood National Park, how can I be of service today?"

"You know I can see you're not doing anything, right?"

The voice was hard, formal, accusatory. It was also a voice Denny hadn't heard in a long, long time. He looked up from the computer screen and almost couldn't believe his eyes. "Chief."

"Don't give me that look, Oh Uh Denny," said Chief Nell.

But it was hard not to. The chief looked so different, and Denny wasn't sure if it was good or bad. "Was your doctor drunk when he reconstructed your face?"

"Fuck you."

"Or did they have to break it again so it could heal better?"

"Fuck. You."

"Quite the potty mouth on you today. Did you learn that from one of the nurses?" Denny smirked and Nell scoffed, shaking his head. "Come on," Denny said, "I haven't seen you in months. I gotta give you shit."

"Yeah, yeah, whatever." Chief Nell sat on the edge of the desk. "Make fun of me while you can."

Denny laughed. "What, are you gonna die soon?" He bit his lip. "Sorry, that was kind of messed up."

"You're not too far off," Chief Nell said.

His face was pensive. Denny could hardly make it out, considering this wasn't the chief's normal glum look. "What do you mean?"

Chief Nell sighed. "I was released from the hospital over a month ago. They suggested that I stay home for at least two weeks, pending how my bones held up after the surgery."

"So they were really bad?"

"No. My face healed early. I felt great."

Denny cocked his head. "What?"

"I felt great, but it was because I was at home with my wife. My daughter came home to make sure I was okay. It was the first time I saw her in months, Denny. I forgot how it felt to not have to hike all day, worrying about burl poachers and making sure you're in line. It felt... good."

"Really? *I* was one of your top concerns?"

"Yeah. For a while, at least. You've shaped up, learned a lot since I took you under my wing."

Denny shook his head. "Sounds like you're getting ready to tell me you're retiring."

Chief Nell didn't say anything, just looked out the window. "Not yet. I'm staying for at least a few more weeks, so I can train the new chief."

That didn't console Denny at all. Although Nell would still be at the park, he probably wouldn't get to see him at all. He would be spending all his time training the next in line, passing on his wealth of knowledge to someone else. Denny wouldn't be surprised if Nell ended up choosing Vanessa to fill his shoes. "I feel bad for the trainee."

Nell's eyes squinted, confused. "And why's that?"

"Because you're a codger who likes things done his way. And you're a shitty teacher." He was trying to cover up his emotions with humor. It wasn't working.

"Well, I guess these next few weeks are going to be hell for you, then," said the chief.

Denny looked up at Chief Nell, expecting to see a shit-eating grin sprawled out on his face. But there was none. "Whoa, Chief," Denny said. "What are you saying?"

"Come on. You really thought I wouldn't pick you?"

Denny's mouth gaped, the reality of the chief's words sinking in. "Are you joking? Because if you are, this isn't funny. Tell me you're joking."

"I am the most serious I've ever been in my life."

He couldn't believe what he was hearing. He just couldn't. "But why? Why me? Why not Vanessa, or Bennett, or anyone else?"

Chief Nell laughed out loud. "Bennett is a dumbass. I don't care that he's being hailed as a hero for recovering the Gerschult burl. And Vanessa, well... she's a good ranger, and one hell of a driver. But she's not quite there yet. You have a knack for the outdoors, everyone who works here does. The difference between you and them is that you have the instinct to not only adore it, but protect it as well. You remind me a lot of myself that way. I see the way you and Vanessa work together, and I like it. I like it a lot. Between you and her, I think I'll be leaving this place in good enough hands."

Denny just stared down at the desk. "You're sure?" he asked, not looking up. "You're sure I'm good enough?"

"No, I just wanted to make you suffer a little bit more before I left." He scoffed. "Yes, Denny, I'm sure. Unless you don't want the position."

Denny's head jerked up. "No, I—"

"I would happily give it to someone else if you weren't up for it."

"I am." Even when he said it out loud, he wasn't sure if he believed it. "I'm up for it."

"Wonderful," the chief said. He got off the desk and walked to the door. "I'm going to be nice and wait to start training until next week, give you some time to prepare yourself. Oh, one more thing, don't mention my retirement to anyone. I'll let everyone know when I'm ready."

"Aw," Denny said, feigning disappointment. "I was going to throw a party."

"I don't want a retirement party."

"No, I meant a 'No More Chief' party. I'm sure people would've loved it."

Chief Nell sighed and opened the door, but stayed inside the cabin. "Get the hell out there. Training starts now."

Denny smiled and sprang up from his desk, holding himself back from launching out the door.

🌲

Sam's head rattled against the window, feeling ever bump reverberate through his skull against the utter silence of the bus around him. He was seated next to someone he didn't know, much like everyone else on the bus. Perhaps some of them knew one another, or had at least seen one another in the past, but the faces that surrounded Sam were all unfamiliar.

He didn't know how this was going to work, or if he would even be allowed to participate. Didn't they know what got him here in the first place? Why would they send him with this group? He decided that he would just keep his head down the whole time, not talk to anyone while he was there. But he would have to talk to someone, right? His supervisor, at the very least, to get them to sign his time sheet. Sam had done the math: at six hours a day, three days a week, he would be done with his community service by New Year's, maybe even Christmas if he found more hours. 120 hours was a long time to go without speaking to the people around him, but Sam would do his best.

The route the bus was taking was eerily familiar to Sam, as he'd taken a similar one just five months ago. The emotions of that day had been lost to Sam's mind, but even so, he began to feel them all over again. Being in the spot that his father was when he was shot. Trying to talk to Bradley and make up for what he did. The fight with Cory. As the bus neared the park, Sam grew nervous, wondering if he would get into another fight today, if someone would start something the way Cory did.

There was a voice inside Sam, telling him it was going to be alright. The only reason he believed the voice—or even listened to it in the first place—was because it was his father's. The bus clunked into the parking lot and Sam pretended not to notice the pit in his stomach.

Everyone filed off the bus and gathered in front of the door, waiting for the supervisor to step out and give them the rundown. The supervisor was stalky, so Sam had no problem seeing him over everyone else. "Okay, listen up," he said, "I'm only gonna go over this once, there's not much to it so we should be fine. We're picking up trash along the trails today, starting here and working our way around. Let's just try and stick together so no one's too far away or anything like that. I'll be distributing bags, gloves, and grabbers on the way out there. Grabbers are on a first come, first serve situation as they didn't supply enough for everybody to get one. If you want one, get one. If not, I don't care."

The supervisor broke through the crowd, fending off people who hadn't listened and were already reaching for the supplies. Sam straggled toward the back of group, not caring if he got one of the trash grabbers. He ended up only getting gloves and a couple garbage bags before he went on the trail.

"As you're working," the supervisor told them, "make sure you're aware of where you are. This is a beautiful place, and you get to be here for free. Just a little something to keep in mind."

Everyone around Sam rolled their eyes or didn't react at all. But Sam found himself to be surprisingly eager to be under the forest canopy again. He'd seen the inside of the same concrete cell for two months without being outside. Sure, there were the times he went out into the courtyard when he felt like he wasn't going to get jumped, but those were few and far between. Plus, there were walls around him then; now, there were no walls. Now, he was free.

Sam bent over and picked up the first scrap he saw, reaching his hand into the garbage bag and letting go. He looked around for more trash, but the vicinity had already been cleared by the people ahead of him. He walked ahead on the trail, picking up every rogue can, bag, or piece of plastic silverware in sight. As he passed the rest of the group, Sam saw people struggling with their grabbers, doing their best to maneuver it into their collection bag. Most of them missed, though, and the trash fell back to the ground. Some of them got fed up with their grabbers and handed them back to the supervisor, resorting to their gloved hand to pick up garbage. Sam felt a little pride in choosing the right tool to begin with, and that was enough to keep him motivated.

Half an hour into their endeavor, the group came to a fork in the trail. The supervisor took to the front, standing next to the sign pointing a different way for each attraction. "We're gonna start with the Ring," the supervisor said. "Follow me."

Sam's heart dropped. He didn't want to go back to the Ring! Why couldn't they go to the Grove, or the Giantess, or anywhere else? Why did they have to go to the place that held so much trauma for him?

The group trekked on down the trail and Sam tried to distract himself from his thoughts by looking at his surroundings like the supervisor suggested. It really was beautiful, the mingling of countless species under one foggy sky. There were trees that seemed to wrap around each other, roots that jutted out of the ground like ginormous veins, squirrels chasing one another from place to place.

Moss covered a downed log, a soft green rug bringing life to an otherwise dead thing. Sam longed to pet it, run just a finger over the delicate carpet, but decided against it and picked up a Styrofoam plate near the log.

Some people within the group were taken aback when they arrived at the Ring. They stared upwards, wondering how a chaotic nature could create something so perfect. Sam wasn't among those people, and not just because he had seen it before. He came to realize that although this place was special, it also wasn't. It wasn't a marvel of nature, something that it tried really hard to do. Nature hadn't tried at all to create the Ring, because it was an accident. Spontaneity was often mistaken for perfection, and Sam wasn't going to make that mistake. Still, he didn't judge the others for looking up, for believing that nature was capable of something like this—they just didn't know any better.

Sam made his way from tree to tree, filling his collection bag with discarded garbage. He picked up a carton of cigarettes, and as he did, he noticed the strange pattern on the tree in front of him. There was an oddly flat bit about five feet up the tree, a bit of bare wood peeking out from behind the bark. Sam recognized the pattern immediately and a lump began to form in his throat.

This is it, Sam thought. *This is the place.*

He knelt down to the ground, his jeans sinking into the damp earth. He knelt on sharp twigs and stones, but Sam didn't mind the pain. It surely wasn't the worst thing to happen at this tree.

Sam took one of his hands and pressed it against the bark, ran his fingers over its ridges. He looked at each one individually like they were mountains weaving up the length of the tree, some of them stopping at the valley where the burl used to be. Sam's eyes were wet, his cheeks soon to follow, until he realized something about this tree. Over the course of its life, it had witnessed countless events, met thousands of people. It had watched someone die in front of it, just after a piece of it had been killed. Sam thought back to Mr. Veranda's lesson about burls toward the end of the school year. He said that they developed whenever a tree experienced trauma, like fire or disease. Even though it was cheesy, Sam believed that trees weren't just affected by physical trauma, but emotional trauma as well. This tree had been through a lot. And yet, here it stood, surrounded by a vast forest, thriving and healing in order to live another day.

There was a tap on his shoulder. "I know it's beautiful," the supervisor said to Sam, "but don't forget about what you're actually here to do."

The supervisor walked off as Sam searched for another piece of trash to scoop into his bag, make it look like he was doing something. His eyes fell on a sheet of bright blue plastic near the tree he was kneeling at. He inched over to it and picked it up, recognizing it as a wrap for a flower bouquet. Sam wondered how it got all the way out here as he stuffed it into his collection bag, the plastic crinkling as it rubbed against the other garbage.

He was alone with his thoughts again, still kneeling at the tree that seemed to be invincible. Were they all like this? Was every tree able to persevere like this one? Sam looked around and saw several downed trees, ones that had given up because the trauma became too much. Even some of the other redwood trees that made up the Ring were looking a bit sickly. What made this one so special?

Sam looked in on himself, connecting the tree's soul to his own. This tree, in nature's infinite improbability, spawned from practically nothing, survived through history, and now towered over much of its surroundings. Sam craned his neck to see the top of this tree, but his eyes couldn't see that far up in the convoluted mess that was nature. Even so, Sam knew that this singular tree was more impressive than the Ring as a whole. It tried to become a giant and succeeded, even though nature had no intentions of letting it do so. This tree had been healed by its trauma—and Sam's. They were kindred spirits, one and the same, sharing the same earth until one of them eventually gave up.

Realizing this made Sam eager for the rest of his life. And then he realized that there was another life he was forever tied to, a soul that, to Sam's knowledge, had not yet been healed.

A life even more deserving of the nickname "giant."

Sam looked around for the supervisor, making it seem like he was just scanning for garbage so he wouldn't look suspicious. Sure, he could just take another trip out here, but what if he really had been banned from the park? What if the tree became infected and died before he got the chance to come back? Sam knew this was his only sure shot, and he'd already decided to take it.

The supervisor was at the other side of the Ring, standing over a small group of people and pointing out piles of garbage. As he handed another collection bag to someone who had filled their first, Sam walked gingerly toward the trail leading up to the Ring, picking up pieces of trash on his way. He got to the trail and walked it back, glancing over his shoulder every few seconds to see if anyone had noticed him. No one gave him a second look, everyone too enthralled in the cleanup effort to care about the one guy slinking away.

Sam broke into a run when the Ring left his sight. He sprinted down the trail, every step sinking into the ground, mud flinging up into the air behind him. The air was nice and cool on his face, countering the warmth he was feeling in his legs and chest. Sam's heart throbbed, shoulders ached from pumping his arms, but the pain felt good; when was the last time he ran like this? When was the last time he *felt* like this?

He came to the fork in the trail and stopped at a totem pole of signs. Sam looked at it for a few moments, eyes scanning them until he found the sign that pointed to the Giantess. He took off down that trail, his breaths syncing up with the heavy footfalls thumping against the ground. They were rhythmic, beating with his heart and growing louder as he neared the Giantess. Sam's mouth dried out from the constant airflow; he could feel his tongue beginning to wrinkle, teeth becoming more sensitive to the chilly fall air. Thin fog crept through the forest as he ran, swirled around him when he darted past it. The sky was gray, the treetops fading into it like skyscrapers in a big city.

Despite the entire landscape looking terribly gloomy, Sam was ecstatic. When a smile appeared on his face, he didn't even want to hide it. The only beings who could see him now were the woodland creatures—and shouldn't they be happy to see him like this?

When the massive tree came into view, Sam stretched his arms out as he ran. He felt like a child pretending to be an airplane, finally letting the whimsy get to him. He spun around in circles, his smile growing bigger and eventually giving way to laughter. There was no one here to judge him now, nothing to force his true feelings to stay inside.

And so, when Sam approached the Giantess, he removed his gloves and pressed his hands against the bark. He let the rough texture stamp itself into his palms, various random lines running up and down his hands. Sam squatted down, not taking his hands off the tree, and touched the bare spot near the roots. Tears began to form in his eyes, his joy and wonder being replaced with pain. Is this what the Giantess felt when the burl was cut from her base? No, it had to be worse. Sam was crying for the tree—something deep down he felt was kind of stupid—because she couldn't cry for herself. He felt terrible about helping Darren cut the burl. Sam didn't really believe in an afterlife, but even so, he hoped that Darren was feeling unimaginable pain, just as the Giantess felt, just as he himself was feeling now.

All the emotions mixing inside Sam dredged up a long-forgotten memory, one that he'd suppressed deep down and thrown to the furthest recesses of his mind.

The small boy walked with his head tilted back, mouth agape as he trudged the trail. His father was a few steps behind, watching the boy's movements and making sure he didn't trip over anything. There were a few times when he had to steer the boy out of a stumble's way, but most of the time the boy managed perfectly well by himself.

"Dad, when do I stop walking?" *the boy asked.*

"You'll know," *the boy's father replied.* "She'll be there, plain as day."

The boy hesitated. "I thought we were looking for a tree. How can a tree be a girl?"

The boy's father laughed. "That's just what they call her."

"Is she pretty?"

"No." *His father looked into his eyes.* "She's beautiful."

The boy smiled, his excitement growing. He had been all for a trip to the park with his dad, especially when he was told that his uncle wouldn't be joining them. The boy didn't like his uncle, hadn't really seen him since he picked him up from school that one day. The boy thought back to how loud and scary that "music" had been, how mad his mother was at his uncle and how much she'd sounded like the man on the radio, screaming his lungs out. The boy was glad his uncle wasn't here, glad it was just him and his dad, going to meet the tallest, most beautiful lady in the park. "How much further, dad?"

"Not too far." *He looked ahead on the trail, squinting and sticking his neck out to the side.* "I think I can see her from here."

The boy searched, but he couldn't find it. "I can't see her! Where is she?"

"Hold on, I've got you!"

In an instant, the boy was whisked into the air and swung upward onto his father's shoulders. He landed with squealing laughter as he perched. "Can you see it yet?" the boy's father asked.

"Nope!"

"Hmm... I think we just have to get a little closer." He lurched forward, the boy almost falling backwards off his father's shoulders. They took off down the path, each of them cheering as they approached the tree.

"Faster, dad!" the boy cheered.

His father picked up speed.

"Faster!"

"Still?"

"Yeah!"

"Okay, hold on!"

The boy's father stamped forward, and soon enough he was standing at the base of the giant tree. He huffed and puffed, catching his breath for a moment before speaking. "Here she is, Sam."

"She's really big."

"Yeah, she is. You wanna get down?"

The boy climbed off his father and stood next to him. The tree seemed even taller than it had before, now that he was on the ground. He was looking straight up and still couldn't see her top. His eyes were wide, gawking at this massive tree.

"Why don't you hug her?" the boy's father said.

"How?" the boy asked. "She's too big."

"That's okay, she'll still feel it."

The boy stepped closer to the tree, looking at the grooves in her bark. He stretched his little arms out to his sides and pressed his whole body against the tree's base. He squeezed, holding himself there for a while to *make sure she felt him. The boy looked up and saw his father moving in to hug the tree at his side. "I couldn't let you get all her love," his father said.*

The boy smiled, happy to be with his father, happy to be hugging the same tree. He didn't know for sure, but he thought he could feel the tree's love flowing through him, a force the moved like blood but was infinitely more pure. It felt warm, warmer than the summer air around him, warmer than the beating of the sun upon his skin. No, the sun could never reach this deep.

He could feel the tree's heart beating against his own.

Sam couldn't believe what he was about to do. But it had to be done. She had to be healed.

Sam stood up and closed his eyes, then stretched his arms out to his sides. He moved closer to the Giantess until his chest was pressed up against her, until he could feel her heart beating once again. He hugged her tightly, his arms hardly even enveloping her huge frame. They were both connected now, the metaphysical string pulling them together until the connection was physical. As he pressed his face against the tree bark, Sam began to cry. He was convinced that her pain was his, that his was hers, and he feared it would be that way forever. But maybe, just maybe, this was enough to heal their wounds.

Acknowledgements

This book was super easy to write, and there are a few reasons for that. First, I knew it didn't have to be big, it just had to get done. I really wanted this to be my first novel because it's such an odd subject that I had tons of fun exploring. I learned so many tree facts, and was even able to insert something I learned from school into the book. Thanks, Dr. Hilgendorf.

The second reason this story was so easy to write is because of my upbringing. I would be lying if I wasn't living and breathing nature from a very early age, and I have my grandparents to thank for that. While my grandpa was out working on the sawmill, my grandma would ask us kids to fill a jug of water and bring it out to him. He would show us how he ran the sawmill, how he split logs, and what he could make out of the wood he harvested. It was a beautiful process, if you didn't pay attention to the mountains of sawdust that lined the narrow walkway through the workshop.

But this story would be incomplete without my grandfather's and father's want for me to follow in their footsteps. Some of my earliest memories are ones where I'm in the workshop, nailing two boards together for no reason. The boards would be riddled with indents where I missed the nail, and my father would call me "Lightning" because I never struck the same place twice. My grandfather was kinder, though, and guided my hand down, told me to never take my eye off the nail head. I was more accurate after that. Without these men and their teachings, I never would have even thought to write a book about trees.

That's where the three names in the dedication come into play. Mark Fischbach, Bob Muyskens, and Wade Barnes have been plaguing my ears for the past three years with their podcast, Distractible. Their grasps on me go even further back to when I was a kid, watching Mark play Turbo Dismount, watching Bob play I Am Bread, and watching Wade be bald. I listen to them almost every day, and their conversations range from camera lenses to childhood fallacies to whether or not a certain something is a cannolo (not a cannoli, that's the plural). But one episode stood out to me among all the others; a bonus episode, no less, nearly lost to time. "The Burls."

I first thought it absurd. How could someone make sustainable wages by cutting and selling bits of a tree? And then I realized, with the help of the Three Peens, that it was crazy enough to work. I can't thank Mark, Bob, and Wade enough for everything they've done for me—and countless others—by just telling stupid stories on the internet. I only hope now I can follow in their footsteps and tell a stupid story of my own.

Also by Zach Boldt

Ties: The Collection
A beautiful collection of short stories and poetry from Zach Boldt's high school years, *Ties* has something for everyone. *Ties* is Zach Boldt's debut book.

From the Footbridge
Moving to a new city can be jarring. Zach Boldt decided that poetry could be his outlet. A great analogy of the highs and lows of life, *From the Footbridge* sheds new light on relationships, mental illness, and finding yourself.

Both books are currently available on Amazon

You can find Zach on TikTok @nacho_doctor_gonzalez